# The
# Sound
# of Many
# Waters

# Short Fiction of Nelson Rogers

"Wedding in the Foothills of Gran Paradiso"

"The House That Jack Built"

"On Eden Lane"

# The Sound of Many Waters

*A novel by*

## Nelson Rogers

This book is dedicated to those from whom I learned between 2016 and 2020.

Words cannot express the depth of my gratitude.

# Introduction

## by John M. Kalil

To truly understand *The Sound of Many Waters*, author Nelson Rogers's debut work, one must simultaneously understand three parallel threads: the author's own personal life which manifests itself in his characters and themes, the novel's profound fascination with the concept of death, and the maze of self-referentiality present in the text that delights keen-eyed readers.

For readers who know the author personally, *The Sound of Many Waters* often feels like an intimate conversation with Rogers about his passions. Indeed, the hobbies and pursuits of different characters closely mirror those of Rogers. In the very opening pages of the tale, Rogers inserts his own love for the instrument into protagonist Martin Turner's dismay at the dust collected on a lovely piano. Then on the train, Turner flashes a keen eye for literature and the work of the greatest authors - specifically mentioning Dostoevsky, a personal favorite of Rogers. Again on the topic of the arts, Rogers and Turner share a love of classical music. Turner himself gushes in his journal about the orchestra performances he attends with the wicked Aesternas, critiquing the various presentations. In short, Martin Turner represents the, shall we say, artistic side of our beloved author. Rogers, an accomplished journalist in his own right, seems to assert his own feelings regarding the obligations of the free press through another protagonist, Hannah Herrman. Rogers served as the print editor-in-chief of his own high school newspaper, the Acalanes High School *Blueprint*. Herrman fills a similar role for the fictional Peter's Post, and even describes a similar work schedule to Rogers. Herrman staying late on Thursday nights to print the paper closely mirrors "work weekend," a monthly ritual at *Blueprint*. So when Hannah explains that in her newspaper, truth "came out in its purest light," know that she is also relating Rogers' own belief in the importance of a free and vibrant media.

But the author's interjections do not cease at the tangible pursuits of his characters. Indeed, a keen reader and personal friend may also detect the insertion of Rogers' own political beliefs. At a political town hall in Reno, Martin's fiancée Virginia espouses the Founding Fathers' belief in a republic and concern for mob rule: "Democracy is irony, and irony is democracy. The people were jousting for their rights, but they so clearly erred in their logic. How can important decisions be left to such impulsive people? I cannot imagine my fate in their hands." Indeed, a keen reader with a knowledge of Rogers' conservative political beliefs and strong support for the United States Constitution will surely recognize Virginia's statement to be heavily influenced by his own stances.

The novel draws its title from Revelation 14:2, found in the final book in the Bible. The reference to a sounding of many waters is also made in Revelation 19. Written by John the Apostle, it describes his visions of God's infinite power and glory, and the apocalyptic end times. The New American Standard translation writes "And I heard a voice from heaven, like the sound of many waters and like the sound of loud thunder, and the voice which I heard was like the sound of harpists playing on their harps." Christianity is a faith engrossed with the idea of death and resurrection, and the Book of Revelation explains in precise detail the kingdom of heaven, as well as the return of Christ which is promised in the Gospels. The souls of the faithful are saved, and the blasphemers of God are subjected to (though not an exhaustive list) scorpions, locusts, storms, earthquakes, and plagues. As for the faithful, "God shall wipe away all tears from their eyes; and there shall be no more death, neither sorrow, nor crying, neither shall there be any more pain: for the former things are passed away" (Revelation 21:4). But those whose names are not in the Book of Life are "cast into the lake of fire" (Revelation 20:15).

Continuing the motif from his title, Rogers carefully inserts references to the ways in which various cultures have pictured death and judgement. As follows is a non-exhaustive preview of this motif. The epigraph is drawn from the *Poetic Edda*, a collection of Old Norse poetry. The selected section in particular deals with the work of the Valkyries. The Valkyries decide who dies in battle and escort the fallen to the afterlife of Valhalla to serve in the heavenly army of Odin. Valhalla was the ultimate goal of any Viking warrior, and could only be attained after an honorable death in battle. The crew in *The Sound of Many Waters* stay at an aptly named Valhalla Inn before the final, fateful confrontation in the novel. Mr. Aesterna's name is chosen with a different mythology in mind. His name of Ozirus is similar to Osiris, the Egyptian god of the underworld. Egyptian souls were said to face judgement before Osiris, who would weigh their soul against a feather to prove the innocence and sinlessness of the person. And while misguidedly snooping around in Ozirus's study, Turner asserts that "I felt trapped within Pluto's gate, the Elm of False Dreams at my back." Pluto's gate is a reference to an old religious site in modern Turkey which was believed to be a ritual passage to the Roman Underworld. The gate entered a cave which emitted toxic gas, leading ancient people to believe in its divinity. Pluto, the Roman counterpart of Hades, rules the Underworld sternly, rewarding the virtuous with eternal happiness and the wicked with punishment. Rogers also makes many other cultural references to the Christian version of death and salvation espoused in his novel's title: The Aesternas own "Vision of the Last Judgement," which was created by William Blake and subsequently lost in 1808. The crew stops in the town Paradiso, a clear reference to Dante Aligheri's third part of *The Divine Comedy* with the same name, referencing the kingdom of heaven. Later in the novel as Martin charts his final designs, he imagines the tenth circle of Hell, which would be below Satan himself in Dante's classic rendering of Hell having only nine circles. Additionally, on a train ride towards the end of the novel, Martin delivers a sermon on the meaning of death and the nature of funerals and remembrance in the Christian tradition. Ozirus has a dream in which he hears the German folk poem "Primal light," which depicts a man's rejection from heaven by an angel. Tracking Rogers' allusions to death and the way in which humans rationalize such a difficult concept is key to *The Sound of Many Waters*.

At its core, *The Sound of Many Waters* is quite self-referential. Various themes and motifs wind their way through the novel and present themselves at opportune times. Indeed, the book often asks questions and then answers them using the very same ideas. A brief notification regarding a few of these things to come is necessary for the casual reader to elevate themselves to that of an expert. At the end of Chapter 2, Turner stares intently at a fresco of an angel with a spear watching a sleeping Christ figure, and says "I could not make out his intentions." That is, Turner cannot yet tell whether the Aesternas are his protectors or destroyers. His question is later answered by a tale told by Hannah's sister Magpie, in which the devil disguises himself as an angel to lure a man towards ruinous temptation. And later, Virginia sees a human form with wings in the clouds, and wonders "was she an angel, or something more devious?" Christian faiths believe that each person has a guardian angel to watch over them -- here Virginia wonders whether the vision in the sky is this guardian angel or a malevolent presence. Her question is answered by the tale's conclusion.

The story of David and Goliath also guides much of the

action in *Sound of Many Waters*. The wicked Father Marquise delivers a homily on the great underdog story (see 1 Samuel 17) which is dismissed by Hannah's friend Clementine. But later, Reverend John repurposes the tale to encourage the journalistic duo to expose the sexual abuse scandal in Marquise's parish, telling them to "find their sling." Then at the hospital in Salt Lake City, Virginia chastises Hannah for agitating Martin and the group towards a confrontation with the Aesternas, saying "Can you see not that he is up against a giant, ten—no, one thousand—times his size? He cannot win; he is but a single man with only us at his side." Echoing her earlier conflict with Father Marquise, Hannah convinces the group to challenge the evil couple with similar language used by Reverend John all those years prior.

The analysis of the bevy of themes, motifs and allusions present in *Sound of Many Waters* could bolster a foreword almost as long as the novel itself. Instead, I leave readers off here to take pleasure in the opening act of a literary career. This profound work challenges preconceived notions of redemption, salvation, and conversion. It transcends one belief system to question the meaning of brokenness and completion, and of sorrow and gladness. Enjoy.

*John M. Kalil is a high school colleague of the author, and a member of the Class of 2024 at Boston College, studying business and economics.*

# Acknowledgements

I would like to thank everyone who so eagerly supported me in the writing and composition process. From my English teachers to my parents and friends, this would not have been possible without your continued support. Creating such a work has always been a dream of mine, and it was only with your guidance that I was able to do so.

Special thanks are extended to John M. Kalil and Jamie Lattin, who so generously took time to edit *The Sound of Many Waters* in its early stages. Additionally, I would like to thank Ariel So for her feedback and comments.

*She saw the Valkyruir*
*Coming from afar*
*Ready to ride*
*To gods people*

*Then appeared,*
*in the field of air,*
*A helmed band*
*Of Valkyruir*
*Their corsets*
*Were with blood besprinkled*
*And from their spears shown beams of light*

**The Poetic Edda**

# The Sound of Many Waters

*A novel by*

## Nelson Rogers

# I

LETTER FROM MARTIN TURNER TO VIRGINIA KELLY

Composed June 6th

Dear Virginia,

Now that I'm aboard the train, I at last have time to write to you. So much has happened in these last few days. Between my employer and new client, it would seem as though the world has presented me with opportunity beyond belief. These last hours have been in and unto themselves an odyssey, which I am more than sure will continue.

Since I left you on Monday morning, I've been through much and yearn to tell you it all. Due to space, I may be forced to abridge some sections of my journey, though I'll be sure the most important parts remain strictly intact. I left the house at just after 7:00 a.m. and arrived at the WINSTON & CO. building not more than an hour later. Upon my arrival, the new clerk, John, gestured for me to follow, quickly I might add.

Together, the clicking of our shoes on the marble floor clapped the rhythm of a gigue. We wound through a labyrinth of steep stairs, winding hallways, and narrow and grand doorways. John, the poor lad, suddenly stopped and stood to the side of the foyer, held open the heavy doors, and allowed me to pass him and enter a large atrium.

I had never before entered this part of the building. My work as a junior associate dictated I remain largely towards the front of the WINSTON & CO. building, and on the lower floors. For signatures, approvals, and assignments, I occasionally visit the second floor. Someone of my level on the third floor, however, was unheard of. How excellent my work must have been to receive such an invitation. My employer clearly spared no expense in this room's decorations, furnished with fine foods and drinks. This was likely where he received important guests. The air smelled sweet like the cherry tarts your mother once made when we journeyed that weekend into the Poconos, but with an additional twang. Though the floor reflected images like an untouched mountain pond, the gray clouds outside the window seldom gave it an image to reflect. The clouds were especially odd, given the season. Twenty-four windows wrapped around the elliptical room. Each window had a portrait of a prominent partner or lawyer from the firm's past beside it. All of them cast their incredulous stares on me. Directly before me hung vertically from the ceiling a large banner spanning at least twenty yards. Made from purple velvet with golden embroidery; it read Finis Coronat Opus and sported a large scale, also embroidered in gold. On one side of the scale was the head of man, and on the other, a flame of justice. Far to the right, a large piano lay sleeping; by my judgment, because of the dust which accumulated on it, it was merely a showpiece... a true shame.

As I concluded my cursory examination of the room, I stared at a large oak table at the center of the room. Around the table stood three men, each fatter and more opulently garbed than the last. They wore three-piece suits, and carried briefcases made from what appeared to be the finest leathers available. Their shoes were impeccably shined, and on those endowed with full scalps, not a hair was out of place.

As I stepped down into the room, their glares caught me like a snare; I was a rabbit in a bear trap. There was no escape. I took my seat with the largest of the men, dressed in a blue-tweed suit, across from me. He eagerly identified himself as Mr. Ernest Shelby with a gregarious grin. His breath stung me as he spoke. It was a scent which I couldn't place, as if I'd once known it, but not in my adult life. I resisted with all my might the expression of my discomfort, pulling in all my face muscles. I did not want to turn away a potential client at the beginning of my budding career.

I recognized the gentleman to my left from my interview with the firm; he was Dr. John Winston Jr., son of the firm's founder, John Winston. Though he was at the helm of the Philadelphia firm's operations, he seemed oddly put-off. His complexion suggested confusion as his brow furrowed. Judging by the extensive notes and paperwork in front of him and strewn about the table, he appeared torn between two sides

3

of an internally destructive conflict. The man to my right, the slimmest of the men, though still quite plump, I recognized only from passing. More than likely he was a partner. His presence at the table suggested he held some kind of substantive power. The way in which he placed his fingertips on the table, palms slightly elevated, thumbs turned inward, led me to believe he had engaged in some sort of negotiation before I stumbled in. His hunch over the table led me to believe he was not winning. Recall you, Virginia, that no more than twenty seconds had passed since I entered the room.

When at last I wracked up the courage to sit among the gentlemen, Dr. John Winston Jr. spoke to me and said, 'Mr. Turner, since you have joined the firm, you have done such great work. I trust that you've been putting in lots of time into your new position (which you'll recall I began only five weeks prior) and I'm happy to inform you,' he began to choke on his words, 'that we've ascertained a new and exciting opportunity for you, one in which you'll truly be able to demonstrate your skill to the world of litigation. Without delay, I'd like to see to it that you return to Chicago with Mr. Shelby and conduct the honorable practice of law,' he said, choking on his words again, like a cat coughing up a colorful cockatoo. He continued, 'For the well-to-do family enterprise which Mr. Shelby represents.' An opened letter sat in front of him, hand signed with red ink. I found this detail unusual, and slightly disturbing. From my distance, with my deteriorating eyesight, I could not make out any words on the page. But I brushed my trepidations to the side in favor of the opportunity before me. As he finished speaking, Dr. Winston lost all color in his face, and his eyes dropped to the table. He was horrified by something, the likes of which I am still at this moment not entirely sure of. But despite his apparent dismay, I found the whole thing very exciting. Seldom is such a young litigator gifted with the opportunity to represent what seemed to be a very significant client. I took it as a personal compliment that I was selected for this... task, and in that moment, I decided I would carry it out with diligence.

I turned to look at Ernest Shelby, who seemed to be gearing up for a long-winded proposition. With the buttons on his tweed suit about to leap off his coat, he drew air inward to begin speaking. I feel he may have procured this particular suit in his youth, as it fit him in a quite youthful manner. As he sat, his waist filled the entire seat and pressed on the armrests on either side. And though his narrow head rose above the top of the chair by a good foot (in comparison to my being several inches below), it was rather small. He spoke and stroked his greasy mustache. It resembled a plucked caterpillar perched above his upper lip: 'I have reviewed your portfolio and work and am significantly impressed by the work you've done in such little time! I'm sure without fail that the enterprise I represent will make good use of your talent, as such an operation requires more than a simpleminded novice; indeed, it requires great ambition. This is a job for someone looking to make a name for themselves, and you strike me, Mr. Turner, as one who wants to make a name for himself. To make matters all the better, I ask sincerely, on behalf of those I represent, that you at once come with me to Chicago so that you might start

Thursday… nay, Wednesday… nay! Perhaps tomorrow! You will be compensated quite handsomely; should you choose to accept, I all but know that your reputation in such a cut-throat profession will be eternally bolstered.' I was very excited at this comment. I tried my best to compose myself and avoid a grin conveying how grateful for the opportunity I was. I had to accept it with dignity and composure, if I was going to accept it with any respect at all.

The partner to my right stared directly across the table. From the looks of it, he desperately wanted to speak. Between his pursed lips and gazes of varying intensity, I was sure of it. Several times his gaze slipped, and his eyes met Mr. Shelby's; immediately Mr. Shelby would return to looking at me, and the partner would return to looking across the table. He wanted to suggest something about Mr. Shelby to Dr. Winston. Though my superiors' expressions concerned me some, further deliberations with Mr. Shelby cemented this opportunity in my mind as one which does not come every day and also was not one for the fainthearted. I did find it curious that no one had mentioned the sector of the economy which Mr. Shelby's enterprise occupies, nor even the company's name. Regardless, I greatly respected the man, mostly because he greatly respected me. He recognized me, and up to that point, I had felt like those to my left and right had not.

As such, I am proud to tell you, my dear, that I have accepted this job, working for a man I know little of and for a company whose name I know not. It is a curious predicament, but after I reviewed the terms of payment, I ascertained that postponing our marriage, but another month or two, will be well worth our while. Always remember, my dearest Virginia, that all I do is for us and our collective future and wellbeing.

So that I could immediately satisfy Mr. Shelby and step into business with him on a good foot, it is with haste I've departed. After our meeting, I rushed home to pack my bags and bid you one last farewell before I embarked on my journey, which by the estimation of Mr. Shelby, should last no more than two months' time. I was disappointed to not find you at home. But I am aware that to request you to change your business for such an impromptu departure would have been quite unreasonable.

With Mr. Shelby's Phantom idling just beyond our garden, I hurried out and neglected composing a letter in the moment to speak of my whereabouts. It is my hope this piece will put your nerves at rest.

The car ride was smooth, and when we pulled up to the train station, a small army greeted us and stole away our luggage so that it could meet us on the train without our effort. Having missed the previous train on the Ohio Railroad by only fifteen minutes (which upset Mr. Shelby greatly), and with another train on the faster Pennsylvania Railroad arriving in just three hours, Mr. Shelby kindly treated me to a nice dinner, though the hour was only 3:00 p.m. As we spoke, several times I tried to inquire about the work which I'd be pursuing. Every time I brought it up, however, he would promptly change the topic of conversation, suggesting we instead speak about our respective educations or interests beyond the workplace.

This game of cat and mouse carried on for nearly an hour before he paid for the meal and we boarded the train. We sat in a special car near the front of the train, and it appeared it was just us in this particular carriage. After a few more moments of stale, superficial conversation—during which his vile breath stung me, and I, with all my might, resisted contorting my face while in his presence—we parted ways. I retired to my cabin and began to compose this letter for you.

I recognize this instance of employment is far from convenient for us at the moment, but should I execute it well—and I'm sure I will if my employer is anything like Ernest Shelby—then the bounty will, by far, outstrip the detriments. We will both be better off because of it.

With love,
Martin

P.S. For security reasons (I assume), Mr. Shelby has informed me that I will not be allowed to communicate with you (or anyone) during this spell of employment, unless it is a true emergency.

### JOURNAL OF VIRGINIA KELLY

*June 6th, Evening*—It has been an entire day since I've seen Martin, and since the morning when I last saw him, my worries have only grown. While I am more than sure he is capable of taking care of himself, I cannot help but think something dubious has gotten a grip of him. His lack of correspondence is disturbing.

The rest of the day has been well. In the morning, I attended my book club with the other city women. Though I hardly find foreign literature attractive, One Thousand and One Nights may be an exception. While the other women took pleasure in discussing its variety of themes and the ancient fables, I kept much quiet, thinking to myself how Scheherazade must stay perfectly balanced on her tightrope of life, with death prepared to meet her should she fail; a proverbial slip of the toe in her stories could end it all. Interestingly enough, however, she escaped the sultan only to live a life which would be met by death—the only certainty whose method and time of delivery is all but certain. I am not sure she ever truly dismounted the rope.

After an hour at the club with the women, sipping cider and such, I attended an hour service at the local parish. It was a large building on Washington Avenue, no more than five blocks from the Delaware. From the parish, I walked on Washington for a few more than ten blocks before I took a right and walked until I arrived at Rittenhouse Square. I always prefer walking to taking the automobile when possible. I find something about the city air refreshing. Though the auto is objectively more convenient, Martin always takes the car to work so I am left on my feet. I suppose my love for the walk is as much out of necessity as it is genuine preference. As I sat in Rittenhouse Square, I watched the birds swoop from tree to tree and listened to the symphony of sounds around me: a chirp, a crash, a clank, a breeze. Does a breeze have a sound? I think so, or rather, I don't see why not. A breeze is a truly transformative thing. All my worries—chief among them, Martin's wellbeing—momentarily blew away. I set my eyes on a ginkgo tree which had recently been imported and planted. In the breeze, it swayed back and forth, and with every lean, it changed shapes. With every gust of wind, I saw a new animal; sometimes it would elongate, and a snake would emerge. This occurred seven times in my counting; other times, a horse would jump from the tree. This occurred three such times in my counting, with another ambiguous shape emerging, which I thought could be a horse. But the wind blew through it and made the quasi-horse much paler. I did not want to rush to judgement, but it spoke to my nature.

From under my arm, I drew today's paper. I read on the front page a headline touting a Democratic victory in the mayoral election. I found such politics rather unexciting, but this recent cycle, ripe with scandal, piqued my interest. It was something to do with mistresses and bribery. I have even heard accounts of men sleeping together! Another story was the recent flight of pilot Charles Lindbergh from New York to Paris, but by this time, the story was rather dated. I longed to experience flight. The freedom, I imagine, would be unmatched. What caught my eye most of all, however, was a report by the Inquirer from Chicago. The recent discovery on the beaches of South Haven prompted a widespread investigation of organized crime, but I could hardly see how the two were linked. I found this headline a bit foolish, as organized crime is an unbreakable problem.

Money could buy anything, it would seem. I'd imagine that silence and compliance are even on the cheaper side of things. No investigation could stop it. But unmatched integrity and altruism... now that could truly put a dent in things, and down such a beast... but even that. Sometimes I wonder. Every time an investigation appeared in the paper, it was seldom heard of again. But one character, so much more noble than the rest... that could make a difference, I think.

I looked up from my paper and pulled my hot beverage from my lips (it had cinnamon... I must remember that for next time!) and with great alarm shrunk briefly into the fetal position on the green, metallic bench as a pigeon swooped from the ginkgo and grazed my hat, pushing it slightly out of position. Its horrific stench momentarily met my nose, and my face contracted. Why this experience resonated with me, I do not know. But I recall a certain excitement during which my heart climbed into my throat... It was thrilling, I dare say. But it passed, and I stood up, straightened my coat, pushed my red hat back into place, and with a dignified breath, clutched my paper and purse and went on my way.

I hope Martin writes soon. While I consciously know he is well in the moment, something is odd; not his absence, but the nature of his departure... yes, that is what's odd.

## TELEGRAM FROM E. SHELBY FOR MR. & MRS. AESTERNA

### Composed June 6th, Evening

I have procured a gentleman. He is young and eager to make a name; he will do well. Took the 7:10 am train out of Philadelphia on the Penn. R.R. and will arrive at the estate by 11:00 pm Tuesday evening. Will not be late. All is well. Dr. Winston has cooperated amicably.

E. Shelby

# II

## JOURNAL OF MARTIN TURNER

*June 7th*—The train ride has been extremely pleasant. Our car was occupied only by Mr. Shelby, myself and an attendant who stood behind the bar and was attentive when necessary. I presume this was accounted for as a business expense, for I cannot imagine the financial burden an entire car should play on an individual's checkbook. And at last, I have placed Shelby's stench to a particular strong brand of suds. Given the time of my birth, in addition to relatively recent legislation and my stringent upbringing, I'd never actually seen the vile elixir. But as a matter of fact, I found it rather repulsive. When Ernest, who remains a true enigma, drank, he turned from a convivial man to a disgustingly gregarious one. He tried for hours to persuade me to indulge in his devil juice. I am proud to say my strong values withstood his test. Our exchange went something to the effect of, 'My friend, you are without bounds at the moment; shed your moral pillars and join me! In this car, the law does not apply. It is not every day you'll receive the privilege of drink while you work; spice up your time on the job—I personally assure no consequences will follow. So long as we pull into the station at a reasonable hour, all will be well!'

'I will certainly not.'

'Take the stick from your behind at once! Enjoy now, for I guarantee you, there will be work for later.'

'No... My values.'

'To hell with values! My friend, I insist!'

'Should my employer find out of my immoral behavior, I should be immediately fired, and my name forever stained!'

'Certainly not.'

'How should you know?' (By this time, Shelby was sufficiently intoxicated so that he might reveal more to me than I should know... I shall probe!)

'Between you and I, I have all but killed a man in my line of work, and the Aesternas have not even flinched.'

'So you justify bad behavior with previous bad behavior!'

'Certainly not! I beg you not libel me like that! I merely reconcile human need with a natural indulgence in the impermissible. Mr. Turner, when I, as an American on loan to the Australians, crossed the River Somme on the eve of August 31st and shot a man, my views on life were forever altered. The fragility of life and swiftness of the reaper...' Upon this note, he leaned away from the bar and fell back onto a couch. He shook his head, side to side, and a moment of silence set in. The suspense was immense, but he spoke softly, 'It's truly remarkable.'

This name, Aesterna, sounded familiar; later, I'll investigate. And though I'm sure his offhand comment about killing a man is merely a clever metaphor, I can't help but wonder, given the quirks of this case, if he isn't lying.

After a moment of solemn reflection, he looked up, and the ambiance of the room grew lighter. 'So who am I to force you to indulge in the spirits of life. If you choose to indulge in reality, so be it!' At this he grinned, stood up, and retired to his cabin without a word. Curiously, as the door to his cabin opened to its fullest, I peered in and did not see a residence, but rather stacks of boxes and another door beyond, which he proceeded to reach for. I found it interesting how without a firsthand account of what lay behind the door, I trusted blindly a man of which I knew little. Alone in the parlor car, I took a moment to browse through my surroundings. I put down my bubbly cola beverage on a gold coaster and looked at the bookshelf below. Whoever had curated the top shelf had a predisposition for grand literature; it was nearly all Tolstoy or Dostoyevsky, with a spattering of classics to the effect of Plato, Aristotle, and Socrates—the biggest names only. The shelf below contained strictly foreign texts, in a language I could not recognize, seldom read. The remainder of the book case contained a smorgasbord of literature, though it was all selected with a clearly refined taste.

I sat on the couch and gazed out the windows opposite. Lights passed in streaks, but time moved glacially. In the corner of the car behind the bar stood the attendant, perched like an owl, mute and discrete. For upwards of an hour, I had forgotten his presence. He wore a white suit, and his hair was slicked back. Though I had not consumed a lick of Mr. Shelby's passion, I felt, by some way of osmosis, looser, and more sociable. I said to him: 'What is your purpose? You stand so quietly, so you must witness a whole host of business. You appear as only a fly on the wall, and if my powers of inference serve me well, then you are witness not only to wealth beyond belief, but also business not known by the common man. Do you know of the task which I am about to take on? Your observations and consequent wisdom must be able to serve me in some capacity.'

'Sir, you must understand a few basic rules about the world you are about to, nay, already have entered. Perhaps most important among them is silence when told. And much to your chagrin, I'm afraid that I've been bound to silence. My lips have been sealed, and the key has been disposed of, deformed, scorched, bent, and torched. While there is much I wish to tell you, and much you ought and deserve to know, I am afraid I cannot be the messenger of knowledge; the repercussions of sharing... I cannot begin to fathom.'

'Well then, when the deed is done and I am on the eastbound train, together we shall toast to a job of the past. I shall sip my cola, and you the finest spirit on your shelf. Together, we will travel to the Orient!'

'In the event such a time arises (he chuckled at this) I would be more than happy to toast, to the Orient! It would be my privilege.'

'It is settled. Now excuse me, today has stolen my

energy and manners. I bid you goodnight.'

It was a most awkward conversation. Much to my personal disappointment, he bucked at the thought of sharing with me the nuances of employment under the Aesternas. Like with Mr. Shelby, I intend to further probe the attendant in a futile attempt to gain knowledge of my task. It has still not been disclosed to me. More and more I am curious of the world the attendant speaks of. With its own rules, as he stated clearly, it continues to sound quite dubious.

JOURNAL OF VIRGINIA KELLY

*June 8th*—With Martin's kind letter, my nerves are at ease; though when he returns, I shall scold him because he has neglected to include an address at which I should be able to reach him. It even looked as though he had written, then erased, an address. I can only hope he includes it in his next communication.

Should he send me an address, I must remember to send him the clippings I acquired from the Inquirer about the Chicago investigations. It may be of interest as he will be litigating there for quite some time.

While my suspicions about the motivation behind this case have not been confirmed, they have surely been validated. I pray Martin has not been caught in a nefarious game, as too often happens to men of decent morals. Both today and Tuesday, I prayed for his safe passage, but to where, I think, I neglected. I should remember this for the next time.

## JOURNAL OF MARTIN TURNER

*June 8th*—So much has transpired in these recent hours. Upon arriving at the train station in Chicago, a small army of servers took our luggage to the car with the same enthusiasm with which they stole it before. Shelby led the way through the station. Its marble floors and shiny countenance reminded me of the one in Philadelphia. Peddlers attempted to sell all kinds of goods, from newspapers to candied apples. Union Station, from my impression of it, had exploded with commerce recently. I recall traveling through on a summer holiday many years before with my mother and sister, but since then the magnitude of business had significantly grown. Though I traveled often for work, the spectacles of cities other than my own persist to amaze. Shelby asked that I pay no attention to the peddlers as it was already late and we had an hour of driving ahead of us.

I walked behind Shelby, which left ample room as his large stature left wakes of people on either side and a vacuum behind, which I filled. Unlike on our train ride, however, he walked through the station with haste. He appeared more focused than I'd ever seen him (though I'd only known him for a notably short period of time). When we finally burst through the doors and into the auto-transit area, another Blacktown car sat waiting. This car was larger than the one Shelby had driven and had two rows of seats. We sat together in the rear.

And there it was again! That vile stench! I may get sick to the core if my sensibilities continue to be offended by its relentless presence. He whispered to the driver, presumably an address. I looked at my watch, and the time was 10:30 p.m. For a large man, Shelby shrunk into his corner of the car; anxiety, it would appear, consumed him. The driver pulled out of Union Station only to be cut off by a large bus. Shelby's anxiety turned to rage as he unleashed all manner of obscenities.

For the first time, I was scared of the man. I had previously been nervous, even suspect. But not scared. I interpreted his ill-temper as a warning; the driver asked Ernest to quiet down, practically putting his life on the line to do so.

We whisked through the city, shooting north on the major roadways. I have been in Chicago a few times and had a basic understanding of its geography. First we passed through Lincolnwood, then Evanston, but this was the northern extreme of my knowledge; beyond Evanston, for all I knew, we were on the tundra. Shelby remained quiet for the rest of the drive.

*June 9th*—The wonders an evening can hold. Looking back, what I was witness to is truly amazing. When, in the cover of night, the black car crunched gravel and slowed to a stop, the driver popped open his door and scurried around to my own, which he proceeded to open. I could see a fountain with a large statue of three dogs, each spitting water from its mouth. Before my shoes had touched the gravel, once again a legion of servers—though this time dressed in formal attire—took our bags from the trunk. I stepped out of the car and what stood

19

before me I will never forget; I could not discern whether it was a mansion of a castle, but it was the largest residence I had ever seen in my short life. I counted six stories of windows, and balconies jutted out at random intervals. Each window was lit such that the house appeared a single room in which the greatest fire known to man burned. Arches to my right framed gravel roadways, and to my left the monstrosity extended until it could not be seen. At the center of it all was a black spade-shaped door, which must have been just more than twelve feet in height. It was divided in half, and cast iron stars, inscribed in discs, set into the door, and fixed to hinges, served as door knockers.

From the chill and humidity in the air, I could tell we were on the great Lake Michigan. But even that was dwarfed by the grandeur of the residence before me. Carved into the stone above the door read Ab Arce Aesterna; Non est ad Astra Mollis e Terris Via.

Once the servants disappeared into their holes and through the arches and the driver followed, Shelby and I were left standing side by side. I took the first step towards the door and he followed behind. 'Have you been here before?' I asked. 'Many times,' he nodded quickly, staring up. This decisive response starkly contrasted his longwinded soliloquies while under the influence on the train. When we stepped in front of the door, he gestured and I took hold of the five-pointed star door knocker. The cold and heavy cast iron geometry chilled me to the bone.

One knock. Nothing.

Another. Nothing. We waited a moment. Another. Still nothing. My heart sped.

Suddenly, the doors creaked. What startled me was not the speed with which the door opened (a heavy door that clearly took strength to control), but it was the sound it made, which brought me back to the earthquakes I had experienced in my childhood.

When this creaking ceased, a stout man, shorter than Shelby but taller than myself, faced us. He wore a red suit and grinned—widely. His black pants reflected the immense light when shone through from behind him, and he wore red velvet slippers on his feet. It was a peculiar, but sumptuous, ensemble, made all the more interesting by a horizontal scar that ran the length of his right cheek and a nose bent slightly to the left—the kind of thing a respectable guest would notice and internally acknowledge, but never bring attention to. He stood to the side and beckoned us in.

I had assumed, with some naiveté, that the exterior of the fortress must be its most compelling feature. I could not have been farther from the truth.

The entry hall was a museum of red and gold. The walls were adorned with immaculate golden features and imposing red drapes hung at set intervals about the round room. The finest Turkish rugs were spread about the floor. Four identical chandeliers framed a square. Together, they gave enough light to brighten an entire castle. Opposite the entry stood eight of the largest windows I'd ever seen. Though I assumed they overlooked the great lake, the scene was shrouded in darkness.

At the moment, they were merely black panels, which sucked from the room every bit of energy emitted by the room's opulence.

The walls and sides of the room held a peculiar mix of art. Four Fabergé eggs rested on quartz pedestals framed by the red curtains. Opposite the eggs on the right wall hung a series of paintings; baroque, romantic, impressionist... the wall spared no expense. At the center of it all, like an iceberg rising from the sea, a slab of black soapstone jutted upward from the floor. It was rough around the edges, but smoothed and shined on its face. It was, by my estimation, a foot thick. At the center of the monolith hung a masterpiece of art which I'd never seen or heard of. It stood five-feet wide and two more feet than that tall. The title, engraved above it in red, read:

A VISION OF THE LAST JUDGEMENT

The gentleman, who I had forgotten was standing to my right, introduced himself as Ozirus Aesterna. 'Welcome! I've heard much about you, Mr. Turner, and I look forward to making your acquaintance better in the coming days. I'm sure you will find plenty of time to peruse the many wonders of this hall and others like it through the castle, as we call it. But at the moment, you look famished and in need of rest. Allow me to see you to your room. I assume that Mr. Shelby has seen to it that you've eaten?' He had certainly not; but at the moment I was not too hungry to begin with. So I responded positively, though I am not sure if I looked Ozirus in the eye, given the entrancing nature of my surroundings.

His name rang in my ears as a curious collection of cultures, and I paid little attention to him beyond the necessary formalities; the majority of my attention was devoted to the continued study of the hall. He recognized this—as I'm sure happens with many of his first-time guests—and gazed with me.

He rested his hand on my shoulder and proceeded to guide me down a hallway located through a pair of double doors in between two of the Fabergé Eggs. As we walked down the hall, I heard melodious tunes oozing from several of the doors. Several of the pieces I recognized as being canon in the classical world. Ozirus observed my observation and commented: 'Pay little attention to the musicians and artists whom you see. We, my wife and I, are patrons for a good number of these individuals; we feel wealth used properly can enhance the value of art in culture. It is a philosophy we live by.'

We rounded a corner and I nearly knocked over a large vase full of yellow flowers. 'Do be careful about some of those things. They're not all replaceable, and I think the Mrs. would be quite upset if some of her collection were to be damaged by a guest. She might be less hospitable... Ernest, this is you.' Ozirus raised his eyebrow and with a tilt of the head sent Shelby through another pair of double doors. Though I could not make out a clear image, a large fire in the background created a silhouette of a figure and a desk. Shelby ducked his head and entered the room. I looked at my watch, recalling Ernest was up in arms about the time at Union Station. It was 12:01 p.m.

and we had arrived late.

'I think you will find that we run a rather militant household,' Ozirus said. 'Though servants, maids, chefs, and the like are subject to rather strict time constraints with occasionally... dastardly consequences; you should know that so long as you accomplish your task in due time, you are subject to none of it. I understand that being away for so long may not be ideal. But I assure you, we are truly appreciative.' He also explained, as we wound through halls, that I should avoid opening doors I was not told to. There were some things which were of the utmost privacy and should be regarded as such.

He ushered me to my room where I found a crackling fire and an expansive bed cloaked in red blankets. In my exhaustion, I must have neglected my evening dress and hygiene because when I awoke, I found myself laying on my sheets in the same clothes I had entered in the previous evening.

*June 10th*—When I awoke, I took the liberty of time to dress myself before I left the room for the breakfast table. On the previous evening's tour, I became quite well oriented with my surroundings, and finding my way was no challenge. I turned a corner and emerged in a large dining room, bustling with activity. There were twelve or so individuals huddled around a single large, rectangular table. I saw an empty seat and rushed to sit before someone else popped out of a hidden door or nook to take it. I turned to the woman next to me for directions about how to order and how one could acquire a copy of the morning paper. She was young, younger than me. A silver bracelet with an amethyst stone wrapped her wrist. She had long eyelashes. Her hair was long, straight, and jet-black. She snickered and said: 'Don't worry about ordering; they'll take care of you. As for the news, you'll find no such thing here; for whatever reason, the Aesternas prefer that newspapers not enter the house. They prefer to keep the artists in a creative box, ironic as it sounds. They don't even have a radio!' This statement perplexed me. But I had not time to give it any thought because a team of waiters, all dressed in the same white suits I saw them in last night, swooped down from the ether. After thirty seconds, a full meal sat in front of me. Clear, white eggs, aromatic bacon, rich French toast... everything one could ask for in one meal. For several minutes, I snarfed down the food in front of me, but not without a composed countenance and collected demeanor. Manners are always penultimately important.

As I pulled a fork-load of toast towards my mouth, complete with butter and syrup, a gloved hand dropped from behind me on my right. It was an envelope addressed to Mr. Martin Turner.

Hope you have enjoyed your sleep and breakfast. Please come see me at eleven so we can discuss your work. O.A.

I had almost forgotten my purpose for coming in the first place! The time was 10:30 p.m. and I could not be late to my first engagement. My eyes widened, and I concluded my breakfast; I needed to prepare my things. I parted ways with

Eluciana, or Lucy Pears, whom I learned in my few minutes of intensive small talk was a world-class trumpeter from New York, who had found her way to the Aesternas via a painter friend and was currently playing with the city's symphony. That friend, however, had unfortunately gone missing in the recent days—present in the morning, and then gone without a trace. All her things, Lucy said, could still be found in her room.

I entered my room and collected my things. I rushed out, neglecting to fully close the door with stacks of papers pressed against my chest and flailing in the wind; I sped through the halls to the office which I had been told to set up in. I walked in at 10:55 a.m. and sat across the desk. No one occupied the desk's seat yet. I was more than sure someone would walk in with folders, papers, and documents at any moment, so I sat upright, prepared for what was to come. I looked up and saw the same novels from the train: Tolstoy, Dostoevsky, and the lot.

A knock, and a twist of the knob.

I was wrong, I could not have been prepared for what I saw.

The person I saw was perhaps the antithesis of my expectations. She was a beautiful woman, probably in her late forties. She wore a black dress with a red band across her bosom. The train behind her was long. And in her right hand, she carried a small rectangular box; maybe an heirloom, or jewelry, or perhaps even part of a body. She walked up behind me: 'I believe you're sitting in the wrong seat.' I immediately moved to the chair to my left and made brief eye contact. 'Perhaps you don't understand; this is your office, and, consequently, your desk.' At once understanding what she really meant, I grabbed my things and hurried around to the other side of the desk.

She brushed one of the chairs now across from me to the side and sat facing me. She stared at me as if to analyze. She continued to do so for a full minute before saying: 'I suggest that you remove your papers,' she said, referring to the wild stack I had thrown to the side without regard for what someone might think of my organizational skills if they saw it. Blushing, I removed the papers and crammed them into my briefcase. The whole ordeal was quite embarrassing. Now that the desk was empty, she placed the small box on the desk. It was like a monument in a desert. By this point, many possibilities rushed through my head as to what the box could have contained: something stolen, a rare rock, a stack of money... I still could not get the thought of a finger, toe, or tongue out of my head. I sat embarrassed, nervous, and blushing like a pomegranate.

She slid off the top of the box. I looked.

I was confused.

'Do you play Five-Up?'

So much suspense for dominoes? They appeared fine dominoes, likely made from the finest ivory given the grandiose of my surroundings, but still, dominoes? I was under the impression this was going to be a meeting of business. So much suspense, so much pressure, all for a petty box of dominoes. Outrageous! I was duped! I stared at her and the box, switching back and forth between the two. She leaned towards me inquisitively.

'Hm? Well?' she said.

Mustering all the formality I had left, I sequestered my embarrassment and nerves.

'I may have played a game or two in my day,' I retorted, as politely as possible.

'Well then, let's begin.'

And so she played out every domino, one by one, and flipped each one over, one by one. All the while, we exchanged glances, trying to penetrate the other's facade. At last we drew out five dominoes. I played the double-six.

As if my embarrassment hadn't been sufficient, she played the six-three, scoring three right off the bat.

She was good.

She then beat me around the post.

She was quite good.

'Domino!' she cried gleefully. I sneered. She laughed.

Needless to say, it was all over quite fast. When all was said and done, she introduced herself. Her name was Ekaterina Aesterna, the wife of Ozirus, who had shown us in. I began to introduce myself before she abruptly stopped and informed me she already knew my name. We spoke briefly of the few hours I had spent in the castle. I said it was a very pleasant place and that the artwork which greeted me was among the most interesting I had ever seen. 'We collect from very (she paused trying to find the words) exclusive sources. Not every day that you come across some of these things. Did you like the Blake piece at the center of it all? It is my favorite.' We spoke for several more minutes about irrelevant things: breakfast, my bed, etc....

'I think you'll find your stay here most pleasurable. There are likely some things you will never be able to do once you leave!' She chuckled at this. 'As for your real work, we'll get to it in the coming days; there is plenty to do, but I am of the mind that you first must be... comfortable within these walls before you begin to spend days in here doing God knows what for some out-of-touch rich folk.' She stood up and began to walk away. 'Lunch will be served at 12:30; I hope you like salmon.' She then smiled a mischievous smile and spoke in a very soft tone: 'And those eggs you saw... well, they're real.' With an excited blink of the eye, she said goodbye and saw herself out.

With forty-five minutes until lunch, I began to compose this entry and reflect on these hectic few hours which seemed like a week's-worth of business.

*Evening*—When I sat to eat, I witnessed a most odd sight: it was Mr. Ernest Shelby at the table. I'd yet to see him there, and he was wearing an eye patch. I took the seat next to him to inquire about what had happened. Though I was not particularly fond of the man, he had been one of my first acquaintances on this odd quest, and I owed him that much respect. He, however, was the first to address me: 'Ah! Mr. Turner! I was just on my way out! I take it you've had a good time.' He was certainly back to his gregarious self.

'Well, yes. I've found the Aesternas and their residence quite hospitable, and among the nicer places I've had the privilege to stay. May I ask what has happened with you? It is not every day a man sustains a wound to the eye that requires him to wear such a... pirate-like piece on his face.'

'Are you well versed with the Bible?'

'Surely, I grew up in a stringent Protestant household. The values have been stamped into me... surely you can remember; though, I have recently slacked in my religious duties. I'm afraid I cannot rattle off verses as I could in my youth.'

'But surely you can recall Proverbs 4:16–18?'

'I cannot say I do.'

'Perhaps give it a read. It will make sense, all in due time. I beg your pardon, but I have somewhere to be.'

He smiled, stood, and left. It was a very odd interaction. It was quite ominous, but Shelby's parting smile was reassuring, as if he knew that I would be safe from whatever malevolent forces lurked about.

I turned to enjoy my meal—a rare-cooked lamb dish with a delicious Texan sauce—when yet another white envelope was delivered by a white glove, which suddenly appeared to my right. This time, the note read:

Hope you'll be able to join us at the orchestra this evening. Car is leaving at seven, show starts shortly after. If you'd like to go, don't be a minute late. I heard they're playing Rachmaninoff tonight; should be one to remember... E.A.

I could not turn such an invitation down. The time was

nearly 6:00, and I surely had to wear my finest attire if I was going to attend such an event with individuals of such clout. I took from the wardrobe my finest tail coat and white silk shirt. I spent a moment before selecting a particularly good-looking black tie, and took several minutes after to shine my nice shoes. A felt top hat and silver watch complete my look exquisitely; I could have been, as far as a stranger was concerned, of the highest social stratum in the country—I looked so refined! With an air of confidence about me, I gallantly shut the doors and began my trek to the car.

My path brought me down a long hallway, which evidently deposited into the entry hall. I looked forward to once again looking at the knickknacks and paintings. But as I did so, I was disturbed by an odd thudding sound coming from behind a wall to my left. A servant girl stood parked like a sentry outside the set of double doors through which I had previously seen the silhouette of a figure, and also through which Shelby had gone in the final moments I saw him on June 8th. She had a stone-cold countenance. I asked her if something was the matter in the room behind. She said I best not meddle in others' business, and it would be best for my own sake that I move along. Persuaded but not deterred, I continued to the car, vowing that at a later time I would investigate.

The symphony itself was among the finest of performances that I have ever seen. Upon arrival, we passed the long line of finely dressed civilians and were brought into a small side entrance, marked with red, velvet ropes. The usher guided us to our box seats. Acoustically, they were not the finest seats in the house, but there is certainly a stereotype which rings true about the type of symphony-goers who line the walls of the great Orchestra Hall. Sitting in our box were Mr. and Mrs. Aesterna, a couple who I did not know (and did not ride in the car with us), a servant I recognized from the house, and myself. There was very little conversation, but from the looks of it, we all thoroughly enjoyed the show; it certainly did not disappoint.

The evening's program began with Rachmaninoff's Isle of the Dead. It was a most terrifying piece of music. It began quite solemn; one could almost hear the oars rowing and the water lapping against the ship as it sailed towards the Isle of the Dead (which was apparently a painting of an ominous rock; though, I was not aware of this until after the show). It was quite magnificent. From there, the symphony moved on to the main course of the evening: Mahler's daunting Symphony No. 2. The program referred to it as the "Resurrection" symphony, though like most descriptive names applied to classical pieces, I feel it was a bit erroneous. It may also be worth noting that within the nearly ninety-minute piece, I likely dozed off some five or six times. But the finale... oh, it was magnificent. Chills, and chills, and more chills! I don't think the classics have ever been so enthralling.

I had a most curious observation, though, when the orchestra stood up to take their bow. Only seven trumpets, while the seats and stands were arranged for eight; the trumpeter farthest to the left from my view was simply gone. The stand farthest to the left was naked on its left side. I found this quite curious.

I looked in my program to confirm my suspicions when I was utterly struck by my discovery. The missing trumpeter was none other than Ms. Lucy Pears, with whom I dined just this morning. I squinted at every trumpeter's face to confirm, but while she was listed in the program as principal trumpeter, she certainly was not on the stage. On the ride home, I confronted Mrs. Aesterna about Lucy's absence, since she was, after all, her patron.

'Oh, you haven't heard? Poor Lucy came down with a case of tuberculosis. It was just this afternoon before we departed. She intended to ride with us, but insisted that her presence in the car and in the orchestra would only serve harmful to those around her. In my humble opinion, it was quite the noble choice, putting others' needs before her own. Quite admirable, if I do say so myself. It would be best if you not prod further, for your own health.' She looked away from me and refused to speak anymore on Lucy's sickness beyond those few vague details. Her sympathy seems quite insincere, and it made me suspicious as to whether her story might be fictitious. I sat back in my seat and felt as if a wall had been erected around me.

The remainder of my evening was quite of the norm, with hygiene, night wear and all. One last note, as I sat in my bed and stared up—I had not noticed it before—I observed the ceiling was painted; it depicted a rocky outcropping, with a sleeping Christ figure in the foreground, and a contemplative angel sitting on a boulder above Him. The angel had a spear resting against his left shoulder. His left arm wrapped around the spear and stroked his chin. He looked down on the Christ figure. Though, for all I tried, I could not make out his intentions. In the distance, I heard what I thought sounded like a faint scream. The dubious nature of this place lingers in my mind. Oh, the evil in the world, I thought, how it always surrounds us.

# III

PHILADELPHIA INQUIRER; GREAT LAKES
CORRESPONDENT, HANNAH HERRMAN;
'UNIDENTIFIED BODY APPEARS ON SHORES OF
INDIANA TOWN'
*As read by Virginia Kelly on June 10th*

*Michigan City, IN*—The body of aspiring Austrian painter Alina Lackner was uncovered by local authorities when it washed ashore on the evening of June 9th. According to the coroner, Lackner had been heavily beaten and assaulted before finally dying from a gunshot wound to the heart. Feathers surrounding the bullet hole suggest a pillow was likely used to silence the gunshot.

The coroner's findings: 'This body at hand is in a most interesting state. The first wounds are from several weeks ago, by my estimation. These wounds had time to heal, while other wounds were recently inflicted. Lacerations on the back have had enough time to scar, but the bruises and cuts around the neck, arms, legs, chest, and head are fresh. Some were likely inflicted between one and two weeks ago, while others were not more than three days old. The fact that the body had been in water for many hours made precise analysis significantly more difficult.'

Opinion of the Michigan City Chief of Police: 'The large span of time associated with the brutality inflicted on Ms. Lackner is truly horrific, and the public can rest assured that the police will do everything in its power to apprehend the culprits of this unspeakable crime. Though, the public should know, the perpetrator may very well lie in a different state, namely Illinois or Wisconsin. The currents of Lake Michigan may have deposited the body on our shores after carrying it a great distance. If this is found to be the case, we may not be able to investigate this crime.'


LETTER FROM MARTIN TURNER TO VIRGINIA KELLY
*(Not delivered)*


June 15th
Dear Virginia,


If you receive this letter, do not fret; I am doing my best to escape the ironclad grasp I am currently in. Getting this letter out of the household will be a feat in and of itself. I will need to sneak it into the mail. All communication with the outside world, I've discovered, is highly controlled. When I was told upon entering this godforsaken place, I was not allowed to write letters; I assumed it was because of the sensitivity of my business, not for the malevolent truth. Speaking of which, I am still yet to have been assigned a task, but I'm sure when that task comes, it will not be of a kind or wholistic nature. Instead, it will be evil—pure and unfettered. Let me tell you of my horrific discoveries before it is too late. My hosts' kindness does little to enshroud their blatant evil.

For several days now, the Aesternas have given me ample gifts and shown me the nicest parts of the city. I have lost count of the number of galleries, theaters, and places of fine dining I have frequented recently. Never have I tasted so many foreign cheeses or acted so socially in my life. But, most recently, I have had to pretend as though I am ignorant to the evil which lurks behind the facade.

It began one sleepless evening when I chose to stroll through the castle and admire the artwork that hung on the walls to pass the time. I passed in front of the office with the large fireplace once again, and I could clearly see Mr. and Mrs. Aesterna imbibing in large leather chairs facing the fire. The bottles were open in plain sight. I observed an entire wall of spirits, scotches, liquors, brandies, vodkas, and mixtures which I'd never even heard the names of. I could not believe my eyes. They were fugitives of the law. They were intoxicated beyond belief. They spoke with no filter. I am afraid to say they were so under the devil's spell, they neglected to notice my presence. Their speech was so slurred, I could hardly make out what they said.

After minutes of fascinated observation, with sudden sobriety, Ozirus turned to his wife and said: 'It is time for you to retire. I have a bit of business to take care of, and I am sure you would not be interested in it in the slightest.' At this, she stood up and walked, or attempted to walk, out a door on the wall adjacent to the fire. A few times in the course of her hobbling and wobbling, she almost fell. When she faced my way, I wrapped myself in a nearby hanging curtain so as not to be seen; though, I am not sure in her inebriated state if she would be able to differentiate me from one of her statues. Once she was clear of the room, Ozirus stood, as if he had had nothing to drink in the slightest, and sat at his desk.

He spun around and opened the large armoire. He emerged from behind the cabinet doors with a telephone; it was modern and sleek, unlike anything I had ever seen before. He dialed a short number and waited for a moment to be connected.

'Hello. Yes. It is he. Okay. How many cars was the train in Battle Mountain? Okay, that sounds correct... And how many in San Francisco when it arrived?... Only seven! That is outrageous; how is that possible? You must realize this is unacceptable! (His face had turned red, and he was yelling quite vehemently). Did you try to bribe them?... How much did you offer?... And they still seized it? God damn! This blasphemous country and its godforsaken laws can go to hell! (Now there was a moment of contemplative silence. Ozirus bent over and placed his forehead between his pointer finger and thumb. His temper subsided.) That must be at least some twenty-five hundred tonnes. Financially, this cannot stand. We'll have to do something about this immediately... I will think of a solution and get back. Continue to try to get it back so long as you don't compromise our identity. So be it.'

He put down the phone and violently hit the desk with his fists. The man was fuming from all sides; it was truly frightening to watch. He stood and walked over to the wall of juice, where he carefully removed a large bottle of vodka. I expected him to reach for a glass and drown his anger in the booze. Instead, he turned around and with an enraged scream threw the bottle to the floor. It shattered on impact; shards of glass shot in every direction and the scent stung me despite my great distance. A proverbial mist enveloped the room. Ozirus sat in his chair by the fire and swore to heart's content.

I was still wrapped in the curtain, and while I had witnessed it all, I was petrified; if I were to be caught, I would surely be punished, or worse. As I reflected, I arrived at the only logical conclusion, and it all made sense. The Aesternas were among the country's illicit alcohol distributors. I had often heard urban legends about wealthy gangsters and crime families. But I could hardly believe it. The Aesternas were so hospitable and kind. Objectively, however, the evidence mounted against them. To my knowledge, there was seldom a business in the country that made its participants as wealthy as the Aesternas. I knew of only a few barons and captains of industry who had attained such wealth; the rest, I thought, must gain their wealth in such evil ways. I thought back to my boarding the train in Philadelphia, how it smelled of alcohol, and how the literature in the car corresponded with that above my own desk in the Aesterna castle. It was the only explanation. I then thought of my career; after working for such a family, would my name forever be stained by the illegality of my actions?

I thought it was the greatest of the evils present in the household, but my naiveté could not have been more. More has happened which time does not permit I tell you, for humans are capable of worse things than the movement of alcohol.

I am afraid that, for the time being, I cannot write any more. I have just moments ago escaped back to my room, and I am afraid of being caught up late writing this letter to you. I will write more to you, if I can find a way to get this letter out. There is far more evil to speak of—but space does not permit.

With love,
M.T.

# IV

## JOURNAL OF MARTIN TURNER

*June 15th morning*—In the hours since my discovery of the diabolic nature of the two Aesternas, I have committed myself to learning how they came by their wealth and evil dispositions. I write this from the train on the morning of the fifteenth, after the previous evening, when Ernest Shelby resurrected me from the bathroom's floor with a sigh and the simple words: 'So they got you too...'

More than I would like to admit, I have snuck through the house, and even into the office once, with torturous consequences. I must record my findings in the event that I am not able to escape this job, which is a reality I have been forced to accept the possibility of.

My journey for knowledge began the morning after I witnessed Ozirus smash a bottle of scotch. I went to breakfast, hoping to find Lucy Pears in her usual seat again, after recovering from her spell of TB, but was taken aback when a new woman, who I had never seen occupied it. I sat down and braced myself for the normal torrent of service. Plate from the left. Juice from the right. Napkin in the lap. As usual, momentary chaos gave way to the finest breakfast known to man. My cheeks were stuffed with eggs like a chipmunk with nuts when the woman to my left caught me off guard. I took a particular disliking to her only for the following reasons, which was likely not proper of me: 1. She took Lucy's seat, who I had recently taken a real liking to, and 2. she embarrassed me beyond belief when she asked me to speak at a most inconvenient moment.

After a moment of chewing, staring, and silence, I begrudgingly met her eyes and asked if I could help her: 'I quite think you can actually. I just arrived here last night and became quite confused. I came to answer an artistic residence advertisement I found in the San Francisco Chronicle. But I arrived yesterday evening to quite a horrific sight.' This piqued my interest, because I too had recently seen a most horrific sight. Perhaps, I thought her account may be of use. 'Before you continue, I must introduce myself. I am Martin Turner, a litigator employed by the Aesterna family from the prestigious firm of WINSTON & CO. in Philadelphia. I've also recently been witness to horrors in this house, and I am of the belief that your knowledge may be of use as I try to shine light on the shadows.'

'I am Danielle Román. I have published many pamphlets in influential writing circles in San Francisco. Though, you've likely not heard my name, since my pamphlets are often too confusing for the pseudo-scholar. Only those with a refined appreciation of literature can appreciate my insights. I would be more than happy to lend you any knowledge I have. Though I have little now, I am certain that within, perhaps... one day, I will have ample knowledge for lending.'

'Given the evils which I have learned pervade this house, any account is likely of use. But here is not the place to speak of them.' I looked at my watch; the time was 9:15. 'After this meal, we shall part ways and convene in my office at 10:00 am. It is located on the second floor in the north wing. I will leave the doors open, so you will have no trouble finding it.'

'Very well. I suppose I will see you then.' With the conversation having reached an apparent climax and conclusion, I stood up and said my goodbyes for the time being.

When I reached my office, I found a folder of routine employment forms on my desk, which I began to fill out. After several minutes of writing, Ozirus walked in to my office and slammed the heavy doors behind him. His countenance was stern and unforgiving. Given my experience from the previous evening, I knew he was at last going to give me work, though I was now more than ever reluctant to accept; I did so out of fear. But little did I know there was much more to be afraid of than a rich man in an expensive suit.

'It has come time for you to begin your service to the house.' He said this gravely, with more gravitas than he had ever spoken to me before. He was no longer a cheerful patron; he was a cynical businessman, out for a profit without regard for the cost. 'I should let you know that you were called here for simple clerical work, but I'm afraid, for better or worse, something of greater importance has risen, and I am calling on you to amend it. I beg that you do not fail, as the long-term consequences would be most undesirable for all of us.' I sensed the blood—the life—drain from my arteries while my heart inched upwards, beat by beat, into my throat, encroaching on my voice. Ozirus looked as though he were about to lunge across the table and eviscerate my bloodless organs. 'You will be traveling to California to take care of business for our enterprise. By now you have surely realized that wealth we have come by is not the most honest or lawful.' I nodded nervously, not knowing whether my agreement was expected or was a condemnation. He continued: 'We have recently had some disruptions to our distribution network, and it is your task to resolve those quandaries. You will be traveling by train, and you depart first thing tomorrow morning. When you board the train, there will a box of folders and files for you to review, specifying the details of your task better than I could verbally in a day. I can nearly guarantee your task will be difficult, almost impossible. But, as in all business, success is reward, and so when you succeed, a handsome sum shall meet you. Please have this done by the thirty-first of July. Ekaterina and I have a small chateau in a little town in the mountains, which we will travel to in the final week of July to inspect your, hopefully complete, work. While this task may seem daunting, I cannot stress enough its importance. We have taken the time to integrate you into this family so that when a time like this comes and we ask something of you that may be challenging, you do it with little hesitation. I beg you do not give us reason to doubt you; I would fear the consequences as much as you. If you have any questions, please show yourself into my study at any point in the day. I'm told that you are familiar with its location, so this should be no problem.' He raised his eyebrows and sent a shock through me. I almost let out a squeak, like a pig at slaughter, neck under the deciding razor. So I knew a part of my fate.

He left, and I looked at my watch. It was 12:13! Nearly two hours had elapsed since breakfast, and I remembered my meeting with Danielle which was set for 10:00. With the doors closed because of Ozirus's presence, she must have not been able to locate my office. So I set out for lunch, and was pleasantly surprised to see Ms. Román sitting in the seat she occupied from the morning. But she was clearly distressed. When turned and her eyes met mine, she stood up abruptly, nearly knocking over her chair. She rushed towards me, grabbed my hand, and violently escorted me into the hallway. 'The devil is here; I swear it.' She whispered this under her breath as we practically ran towards her room. She suddenly stopped and said to herself, 'No, no, no... They'll think to find me there,' then she turned to me. 'Where is your room? We must go there at once.' And so I, with Danielle in tow, hurried off to my quarters. Once the doors were shut, she spoke with a great deal of panic in her voice: 'I do not have long, and I'll need to escape at once, but before then, I am going to recount for you the two greatest traumas I have experienced since my arrival here. The first was when I arrived. As I stepped out of the car which picked me up from the train station and walked towards the house, there was movement in the shadows under the arches in the driveway. I stopped for a moment to look, as one does when one is hiking and they feel a coyote or mountain cat is stalking them. I made out a group of figures, whom I later confirmed were among the staff and servants in the house, carrying a heavy blanket folded in two into the garage. It was all well and good until a saw a foot peek out at one end of the blanket. I was momentarily horrified. At first I doubted my intuition, and soon after convinced myself the foot was a figment of my imagination. I continued to doubt myself until this morning. I entered the north wing on the second floor expecting to find the double doors of your office open. Finding no doors in such a position, I narrowed my search to two pairs of double doors, given the labels that accompanied the others. So, believing that the first pair of double doors was your own, I showed myself in. (I was very nervous at this moment, since I knew what was behind the doors she spoke of: the study of Ozirus Aesterna). Martin, what I saw is unspeakable. It is the most awful manifestation of evil I have ever seen. Standing in a circle were the same servants who carried the blanket—nay, the body—to the garage. When they noticed me, they stood to the side.' Her speech became frenetic: 'Opposite me stood a woman of medium height, wearing a matte black dress. Her hair was pulled back, and her eyes were red with rage. But most frightful of all was that she was covered in blood. She wore gloves which came up to just below her elbows. I could tell they had once been white, but in their current form, they were a gradient of red; the hands were soaked in the stuff, while streaks of it ran between the ends of the glove and her arms. Blood dotted her dress and dripped from her chin. Their cultish gathering oozed Pagan witchery. I lost all sense of time and was scared beyond belief.'

'When the she-devil's eyes met mine, I knew I was in danger. I turned to run, and she scowled something which I could not understand. I made it out of the room before anyone could get their hands on me. But, Martin, I am now convinced that I am no longer safe in this house, nor was I ever. Sitting to wait for you in the dining room... I've never been so fearful. I must escape immediately; I cannot even go back to my room. I ask that once I am gone, you do me the favor of retrieving the manuscript of the novel I am writing. I consider it my masterpiece and am greatly disturbed that I must part with it.'

I assured Danielle that if the opportunity presented itself, I would retrieve her manuscript. Though I also informed her that I would be leaving the next morning on business, which she half ignored. I thanked her for her accounts. Without another word, she left my room, and I have not seen her since.

I was more curious than ever. I recalled Ozirus's invitation to see myself into his office, and I was now more than ever eager to do so. Quietly, I traversed the castle and saw myself into his study. When I entered, I looked around to see if any others were present. I was pleasantly surprised when I found that was by myself, though secure with my employer's blessing. At last I had time to explore the study, which I had only seen glimpses of in passing and through the curtain.

If the entrance hall was an ornate and curious

collection of art and artifacts, then the study was the entrance hall, scaled down several times, and with several times as many artifacts. It possessed all nature of worldly things: bronze and jade sculptures from the Far East, tapestries from the deserts, and paintings from Italy. Despite these wonders, a large leather bound book sitting on top of the bookcase caught my eye above all else. On the top, it read A Familia History de Aesterna. Though I had never strongly taken to Latin during my time in grade school, I had intuition enough to realize this great volume contained the Aesterna's family history.

I am not sure I have ever wanted to read such a daunting tome as much. Careful that all the doors into the room—of which there were several—were shut so that no individual could sneak up on me, I opened and began reading. I shall summarize my findings here, as they are most interesting:

1614—E.B. dies near Višňové; I had never heard of this place, but there was a great deal of detail on this event. Though the man behind the initials was never revealed, to my knowledge, he was quite the murderer of his day, a tendency which I suppose has been passed down. This figure lived many generations ago, but it would seem that whoever this 'E.B.' is, he is the beginning of all things significant.

1701—Ancestors relocate to Eastern Europe and take the surname "Aesterna."

1853—D.A. marries wealthy Egyptian trader; here it seems the wealth of the family increased greatly, as the tome begins to list the family's various holdings throughout the known world.

1900, or near the turn of the century—V.D. dies; he was evidently a great war hero based on the ample praise of his skill and valor on the battlefield. Though V.D.'s death seems like somewhat of an anachronism, out of place in time given the wars the tome enumerates. Like the mysterious E.B., V.D. is quite an evil figure.

1902—O.A. marries E.D.; this I assumed must be the marriage of Ozirus Aesterna to Ekaterina. Her maiden surname was not listed.

1911 January—O. and E. immigrate to the United States and open fiduciary business, serve many wealthy clients.

1911 November—O. and E. buy lakeside residence and meet and engage in business with M.W.; this was very dubious. The ambiguity of the term 'business' was overwhelming.

This was the extent of the important information which I felt pertinent to my quest for knowledge. While there was no great detail, and no secrets were uncovered, I learned of the family's murderous disposition. I was now frightened to be in their presence. I felt trapped within Pluto's gate, the Elm of False Dreams at my back. But as I turned to close the book, a piece of tattered parchment fell from the worn back cover. It was a letter from Ozirus to Ekatcrina, dated in April of 1911.

*Kat*—I wish to tell you a story from my youth. Once, when I was only nine, I was in Egypt visiting my grandfather. Our caravan took off from Cairo, but my grandfather had abandoned civilization in favor of a small house in the desert. We were forced to ride horses, as there were no paved roads that took us to his residence. But a monsoon set in, and my father and mother died in the storm. After two days of rain and thunder and lightning and the unfettered rage of God, I was alone with only one horse. So I walked through the desert on this horse while the sharp beams of the sun struck the moisture flat. For days, I was stranded drinking what little water I had left. I sat on top of a horse which I could not control, in a country I knew nothing of. But there was a serenity to it. It was peaceful without the strange nags of life. Eventually, I came to a dried river; it must have once been great, because the slit in the earth was wide, with ample sediment below it. I was saddened by the thought that once a flourishing river had died, and the life with it was gone.

But a group of traders found me. Without realizing my family's standing in society, they kindly brought me back to the city, where I was able through a string of fortunate events to reach my grandfather.

Ekaterina, we have been through the desert; we have been rocked by a storm; and we have been found by some traders; I beg you come to Chicago so that we can find my grandfather. I have done all I can, so we can be happy. My work has now paid off.

Together, we have been through much. I know your father was a brutal man. I know executions and tortures and even the gallows were common sights in your childhood, as they were in mine; together we have seen the blood of a thousand men pour out onto the battlefield. But I consider this no handicap; instead, we more than any others in this life are blessed with the ability to be ruthless, cunning, and cynical. We are not bound or boxed by the moral pillars by which others live. We are our own gods and together will acquire wealth which simple men cannot fathom.

O.A.

This piece disturbed me greatly, because it confirmed my suspicion that Ekaterina was the she-devil Danielle spoke of so horrifically. She had been born into gut-wrenching conflict, and it was not reasonable of me in any capacity to think she could possibly change that. And meeting Ozirus had not only enabled her growth as an instrument of evil, but it encouraged it. The cliché goes that some couples are matches made in heaven, but this one was surely from hell.

As I was assembling the book back into its original state, I heard a door open to my side. Framed by the light stood the couple, Ekaterina in her usual tight black dress, and Ozirus in a red corduroy suit. I just short of fainted. The blood rushed from my face as I stared death in the eyes. 'I... I... had a... question.' These were the only words I could eke out before Ozirus spoke: 'I am sure you do, but know that you are not a guest but a worker of this enterprise. You are not gifted the same leniencies. What is your question?' I was paralyzed. My lips quivered, and my hands shook. My lungs froze as their vision cut through my guard like butter.

Ekaterina spoke: 'Seeing as you clearly have no

question, I am forced to assume you were snooping, which is a most deplorable crime. I am going to have to ask you to follow me... (I stood frozen paralyzed by fear)... NOW!' she screamed. Ozirus slapped me across the face. By some means, I regained my bearings and walked to him like the decrepit being I had become.

When I walked into the room, a sickening, sweet, metallic stench stunned woke me from my paralysis. I abruptly turned and vomited on a chair. Another slap across the face.

The only detail I can recall with utter certainty was a silver bracelet with an amethyst stone embedded in the center. It struck me—that Lucy had not been silenced by tuberculosis. The only disease she experienced stood over me. I'm afraid I forget the precise details of the room. I remember lights and mechanical sounds. I remember lying down. But soon after, I was lying in my bed and the time was 3:00 am.

The entire episode seemed like a bad dream. But when a stripped down to bathe away the stench which hung around me like a cloud, I realized I had had no dream. I, like Lucy (God bless her and her friend before her and her countless friends before her), was a victim of Ekaterina.

Standing out of bed, my side ached and I was weak. When I passed into the bathroom, leaned my entire weight on the counter and looked up, I saw the reflection of a ghost. I was gaunt, all color gone from my skin. Taking off my robe, the single article I was dressed in, I observed six large gashes in my side. Gripping the tiles, I began to cry. Tears rolled down my face, and I sunk into the floor. I clung to my knees and let the tears flow. As my knees came close to my face and my back stretched, my wounds opened and blood seeped on the floor and into the tile grout. Across from the counter and above the toilet, a miniature print of God the Father watched over me. The pity in his eyes was unparalleled. I was a proud man in a well-to-do family with a future before me. But vanity got the better of me, seized my aspirations and left me collapsed in a pool of blood on the bathroom floor in the house of murderers and bootleggers. I reached for the bottle of whisky placed on the counter above me, and, in my crazed state, imbibed to calm the pain. As the heavens rained pity and washed my tears away, my body gave way to a snake-stricken heart. I passed out in complete exhaustion.

# V

## DIARY OF HANNAH HERRMAN
## 1902

*December 15th*—In all my years at the St. Peter Day and Secondary School, I have never known such an exciting day. For years now, I have toiled for that little school paper, so much that it was really the only thing I had. Our Colored school on the outskirts of Baltimore hardly received enough money to keep decent staff, let alone a new age luxury like a printing press. But now, the days are gone for those of us who have fought with odd machines and presses to print our paper.

But *Peter's Post* was not just for our little school. The whole town relied on it. For years we have had to stay late Thursday printing and printing and printing. The process was eternal. Then, come Friday morning, we would have to arrive hours early to school. Each of us who, every week devoted hours on end to our little labor of love, mounted bicycles, scooters, and our own worn feet to distribute our town paper.

In many ways, *Peter's Post* was the pride of our school. I had grown up seeing it distributed as a pamphlet around the courtyard. Then, when I was in the sixth grade, Jeremy Smith was the Editor and had the genius idea to distribute it to the people of the town. And they ate it up. All the big papers overlooked our small enclave of civility. Though we were surely a city with a fine little post office, we were just a hair too close to the countryside to be considered urban enough for something like a paper. For the citizens, it was a time for gossip, and the truth came out in its purest light.

The White schools, about twenty miles to the East, had their own little paper, and they had more money and better pictures and such, but in the minds of the town, nothing, not even The Times, held a candle to our dear Post. Perhaps it was the fine journalism, or maybe it was just that they appreciated reading about themselves; after all, the town was small enough that if, in the course of a year, others did not read your name in print, people mind go knocking on your door to see if you were alright. The big papers seldom reported on our little black community. So when we had the opportunity to showcase the labors and toils of the blacks around us, I did not know a single person who was not better off because of it. Everyone knows everyone, and everyone likes knowing everyone. It is cozy, and it feels safe.

And now that we have our mimeograph, our job got a whole lot easier.

I hardly expect much when I get to school on Monday mornings. But today, something in the air was different. Maybe it was because it had rained the previous evening, and the asphalt had a pungent smell, or because the clouds had parted and what few flowers remained opened themselves to take in the jovial rays of the sun.

When I got to the school building, I entered through the front, as I normally do, and noticed a crowd of my friends, all in their uniforms on their tippy toes, huddling around a table in the writing room. Intrigued, I walked in. I walked faster and began to hear awe in their voices: 'I've never seen anything like it,' Clementine said. 'I didn't think that we'd ever be able to get one of these,' Walker whispered. 'Where do you think they found it? Who had the money?' Hale said. Then, as I peered over their shoulders, I saw why their jaws had become unhinged.

The aforementioned mimeograph was a beacon of light in and of itself. Looking at it, the advances of mankind glowed. It was the epitome of modern technology. It was sleek, and it was shiny. It sang to me in its sharp inanimate way. What rendered me speechless most of all, however, was the fact that we had it. New-age machines like these, I thought, were reserved for the White schools that could afford them. Many times sitting at the writing tables hitting our clunky, old presses, we had optimistically joked of something like it. And we knew the machines we dreamed of existed, but we never in our wildest imagination thought one would ever land in our laps as beautifully and plainly as it did this morning.

The morning bell rang, marking 8:00. We all realized we would soon be late for class, so made a point of dispersing quickly. Though, those twelve of us who produced *Peter's Post* and knew the true value of the little machine walked away without taking our eyes off of it, until the very last moment when he had to duck behind a door and rush to class to avoid a whack on the knuckles. And so our morning classes elapsed and we had our lunch, which we spent, once again, fantasizing about the little machine—but it was no fantasy. It was truly there. Perhaps it was our fantasy. But is it a fantasy in the event that it come true? So we pondered that. Then our afternoon classes elapsed and, while most of the school rushed out of the main hall and towards the safety of their mothers, the rest of the Pete's Post People (as we liked to call ourselves), assembled in the writing room, this time with Ms. Booker, the writing teacher who coincidentally knew how to work a great deal of machines, to take one last look for the day. She spoke sternly: 'Now, I know that you are all likely quite eager to begin turning the wheels on the mimeograph (she could tell from our smiles; I knew it), but it is important in times like these not rush, and take our time so that we can use the machine the right way. So we will continue to press until the New Year, and then, only after winter session, will we begin to print like has never been done before.' Even she cracked a smile at her last sentence, and she was a very stern woman. So all of us went on our ways.

Since no one had interviews or writing they had to do for *Peter's Post* today, Ms. Booker locked the writing room, our prized possession within, and sent us all on our way. Hale and Clementine went home to help with house work, Walker went to help his parents in the general store, and I, realizing I had stayed just a bit too late for my own wellbeing, rushed home to take care of my sister. The walk home today was not too atrocious; although it rained, the morning hours of sunlight did well to reduce the mud to mere wet dirt, so I skipped from patch of grass to patch of grass, like a frog jumps from lily pad to lily pad on a serene spring pond.

But as I skipped from pad to pad over puddles, a black plume caught my eye in the distance. I could not tell the source because the trees stood too high, but a fire had erupted, and was raging in the distance. I was not sure what was over on that side of town, at least not in the day. My friends and I seldom ventured there, except at night when we escaped our houses (much to our parents' chagrin) and went exploring, as we called it. I knew it was poorer than the rest of the town, and more forested too. From the few times I had been, I knew there were no lanes of houses or white picket fences, but neither were there anywhere I lived either. Instead, there were long roads which winded like snakes through the forest and over rivers and across fields.

So I stood there and took a moment to be sad for whoever's house was burning down. The thought crossed my mind that maybe a campfire had gone rogue, and sent sparks into the air and nearby trees, but I corrected myself—no, of course it was a house fire… that's the only kind of fire we ever really see here, the kind that kills someone and their livelihood.

*December 18th*—So came that time of week today, when we,

Pete's Post People, stayed our hours after school, setting up the machines and pressing the ink into the paper and folding hundreds upon hundreds of little pamphlets. Our press at the time could not handle multiple pages, so we were only able to print on one side of a sheet.

This would, of course, all change with our new machine.

Our headline this week was about the town's Christmas decorations. There was never too much new which happened in the town, so more often than we would like, we find ourselves reporting on things which do not meet the modern definition of news. But there were lights that were going up, and for the first time ever, we were getting a town tree. It was to be erected in the center of the square, so that when winter session began, every child and adult and family could bundle themselves up and sojourn to the epicenter of life here, and sip hot cocoa and coffee and teas at the shops and stands which inevitably surrounded the tree. Under the colorful lights, all few thousands of us would have an experience, one and the same. I know it sounds like somewhat of a romantic fantasy, but most people here are really of the mind it is possible, and that this year would be the first.

So we each took turns pressing and folding and tying. Occasionally, I found myself without work, so I took a step back and admired the well-oiled machine—which we took so much pride in—and had created for our little school. On the walls hung some of the most important papers we had printed in recent history. The most important, if I recall correctly, was the paper from the day after Roosevelt won the presidency. I was in the eleventh grade, and so many people clamored for a paper that we ran out within the first ten minutes of standing on the cold corners around town. I remember it being especially tough that week because no one wanted to wait until Friday, so when we got word on Wednesday night (because the communication could be quite slow to the town), we stayed up into the early hours of the morning printing and folding and tying. We stayed so late at the schoolhouse that parents began to show up in pairs wondering if their kids were still alive. Once we assured them we were safe, we spent the night there, all of us together. And it was most fun, I think, I had ever had. Sharing an experience like that, I think, is good for the mind. It lets you take the world off your chest and talk freely.

But based on the past, I knew tomorrow's paper would not fly out of our hands. People would take it, slowly but surely, and pay their five cents and move on with their day. Passersby would recognize the homey staple and warmly accept a paper with two hands and smile with a little nod of the head. We would smile back, and they would pass on into their lives, leaving our little sphere of acknowledgement, where we were momentarily shielded from the evils of the world. Tomorrow, as always, is going to be a hoot.

*December 19th*—And so the morning came today. We arrived at the writing room at 6:00 and were in our places by 6:45. As usual, people began to emerge from their houses and walk to the center of town. They picked up their coffee and their paper, and they went on their way. Since it was winter, no one walked on Country Lane out to the fields. Instead, they jumped into buses to be taken to the nearest factories. It always pained me to think that we maintain our little economy enough to allow people to do their work in town. The money just was not here; it was in the cities in the hands of people who wanted to spend it in the cities. We were a backwater of Baltimore, but then again, that is just always how it had been.

# VI

## DIARY OF HANNAH HERRMAN
### 1902

*January 15th*—A new boy came to school today. It was unusual. There has always been a fair amount of turnover in our small class. The town had, in general, a relatively transient population. One day, a new girl would arrive, and we would become friends. A week later, she would leave and I would be all alone again. My parents came to Baltimore in the late 1800s for the schools, and I was perhaps one of three students who had been at the Saint Peter Day School since the first grade. When they had come, my parents had very little, but through sweaty labor had gained enough money to provide my younger sister and me a pleasant childhood.

They spent most of their adult lives working to provide for us, and I respect them greatly for that. I have accepted, and I try to impart on my younger sister, that we must work hard and make good use of the God-given childhood which we have been blessed with. Our house was not large, nor was it spacious. But it had a warm hearth, and when our family sat together, such a hearth was all we truly needed. And there was little free time. I was a diligent student and determined young woman. I was going to have a future; I was sure of it. My years of play had elapsed, and I needed to mature or be eaten by the world, chewed up by its sharp, shiny teeth.

I have always been quite proficient in my studies, and my parents tout that they have no shortage of praising comments from my instructors, in all subjects. I can read and write and compute and think just as well as any white girl my age, and better than most of them, in fact. But we are not allowed to be educated with them. But in my class today, this new boy, Arthur... his mind challenged my own; but I liked him, and I sensed he liked me. He was much younger than the rest of us in the twelfth grade, and an aura of innocence followed him like a ghost.

Most remarkable of all about this little boy, however, is that he was white. It shocked all of us, who had only been schooled with other blacks. His presence confounded all of us, with no exception; what, we all wondered to ourselves, would a young white boy with smarts be doing in the colored school system? Heaven knows that the white schools would serve him better not only in terms of his education but a career.

But little Art (we all called him that) seemed to enjoy his day. The teacher would call out a problem, and he would be the first with his hand up. My observations of him on this day pinned him as smart, but naïve. During recesses, while the rest of us leaned against the walls, sat in circles, and gossiped about whatever was going on that day, he would draw himself boxes for hopscotch and run around for no apparent reason. No one paid too much attention to him; there was no reason to. He stayed mainly to himself and never asked for trouble.

When I got home that day, I went through my usual routine of diligently completing my assignments, and picking up and watching my little sister until mother and father came home once the moon had risen. We ate chicken that night, but my arithmetic was so engrossing that I neglected to take it out in time; so Magpie and I ate burnt chicken washed down water—a more than typical meal for a more than typical night.

After dinner, I curled up on the couch, with Magpie (her full name is Maggie Pauline Hermann, but she was so talkative and father loves the damn birds so much). We made up stories for one another; sometimes they were ghost stories, and sometimes they were romances, and sometimes they were most thrilling tales I have ever heard. Magpie had a natural knack for telling stories like that. She is the most crafty and creative little girl I know. From age two, she could see herself in the mirror, and by age three was speaking the Gospel.

But the story she told tonight was so horrifying and mature that I question the depths of her mind and wonder where it came from. Together, we have read many books. I read to her, then she insists that it is her turn to read; she'll read a page, then I'll finish the chapter. Father travels often to New York, and since he knows of our love, he brings us the most exotic and fantastic tales, all beyond our dreams. The story that has always fascinated Magpie and I above all others is Dracula. We must have torn through the poor paperback ten times. Every time the count approaches Jonathan Harker with a child squirming in a bag, Magpie curls up next to me real tight, and asks if the child will be okay. I am not sure how I respond, usually I dance around the fact the child will surely die, and in a most gruesome and horrifying way. Maybe it's from this horrific text she found her story. But I can only hope it was not an absolute original. It goes as follows:

Once upon a time... (Magpie always began this way. I chastised her for the cliche; but that is probably the only reason she did it) there was a man, who lived in a log cabin one-hundred miles from the sea. But one day, his wife fell ill and was forced to her bed. After one week, she became so sick that the man walked one-hundred miles to a town near the sea to find medicine and seek the help of the doctor. But along the way, the man met more women and fell in love. He felt immense guilt, but never called off his newfound love in the town by the sea. The man chose to spend the night in the town by the sea, thinking that his wife, whom he left in perilous condition, would last one more day.

As the man lay sleeping, the sea breeze enveloped him. It surrounded him and lifted him into the air. While the man slept, nature whisked him away to a cloud, where he came to sit. When he awoke, he sat on the cloud across from an angel dressed in a blue robe.

'Where am I?' asked the man.

'You are in a difficult place,' chuckled the blue angel. 'You have before you a choice. You may stay near the sea for your life and receive all the worldly pleasure one could ever want (I was truly shocked at this) or you may return to your wife, comfort her in her final moments, and live a life of solitude and remembrance. She will die, and your choice is simply to see her to heaven as you're perhaps obligated, or allow her to embark on the journey alone and live your life by the sea.'

The man thought, and the angel stared. She will die, and she was a good woman and wife, so my presence in her final moments will make no difference, he reasoned. So the man told the angel of his choice. The angel nodded.

The blue angel took the man back to his bed. But then a most curious thing happened. Instead of flying high into the sky as angels do, the angel grinned a most cynical grin, showed a mouth of gnarled and fanged teeth, and melted into the ground. The man was frightened beyond belief. The next day, the angel set fire to the cabin, and the smoke from the blaze consumed the town. His wife's death tore at the man's heart, ripping it from his chest.

For many years, the man lived peacefully. Until one day, in his old age, the sky spoke to him and brought him to purgatory. As the man entered, he looked down and saw the blue angel staring up at him with fire in its eyes. As he was sentenced, the decider held up his heart, which had been taken from the man's chest. And with that, the man knew his destiny. And so the blue angel flew up from the depths of hell, grabbed the man by the ankles and pulled him down (Magpie jumped to the end of the couch and grabbed my feet).

He screamed, but no one could hear him, as if the water from the sea silenced his cries.

The end.

When Magpie finished, she had a smile from cheek to cheek, and she knew that her story had jarred me. My mouth was open in an awful combination of amazement and disgust. She had, at least temporarily, deprived me of the will to tell her stories with that horrifying tale. So I sent her to bed, and still in awe, began to chart my day's events.

*January 20th*—Little Art kept showing up to the school, and kept minding his own business, and kept excelling in his math. Today, though, I decided to approach him. Seldom were the children who attended Saint Peter's Day school so gifted, let alone white. He had one foot in square eight and one foot in square nine when I came to him. I think he waited because he had slipped jumping onto square ten several times, given the ice and snow. I do not think he expected anyone to speak to him, because when I approached, he stared at me, not in a loathsome or hateful way as I have experienced, but in an inquisitive and curious way. He stood in squares eight and nine for a full minute, and his eyes glazed over. 'Little Art, are you in there?'

'Yes, yes I am,' he said as he regained his dignity. I do not think anyone besides the instructors had actually spoken to him since he arrived, and this interaction was all new.

'You've been doing pretty well in your schooling. You like to learn especially?'

'Eh. I try. Sometimes.'

'Well, where do you come from?'

'My parents came here from a little town in Pennsylvania a long, long time ago. I don't know what it's called, because I was really little when we came.'

'So then where did you do all your learning?'

'Mainly my parents. Sometimes my grandma. Whoever I am with at the time. But they say it is time for me to do go to a school with people.'

'What do you mean whoever?'

'Well, sometimes my parents are here, but then they leave. And then Grandma shows up and will teach me to add. And then she leaves, and my uncles come, but, eh...'

'Well, that's a lot going on for you. Do you stay in the same house?'

'Sometimes. Sometimes I sleep in the house and sometimes, I sleep in the shed. It is always up to whoever I am with at the time.' I found this comment particularly interesting.

'You mean to say that sometimes you sleep in a shed?'

'Well ya. It is not a lot. Mostly always when my uncle is here, and he says it is for the better, but it gets kind of cold sometimes.' He spoke as though his experience was a fact of life. There was no sadness, but a bleak acceptance of reality. It was his normal, and it shocked me. Our conversation took an unexpected direction. But I was curious to see where it would go.

'Well, little Art, who is staying with you right now?' Their family situation seemed complicated, and I could not comprehend its nuances, but knew enough to ask.

'Gran died, and ma and pa said they'd be back in a little. They took the body.'

'You mean to say that you're all by yourself?'

'I guess so.'

I was astonished. He was a young boy who could not have been more than eleven years old, and his reality was a lonely one. My heart ached for the child, who had truly never experienced the wonders of a family. He lived by himself, with only his mind to occupy him.

'Little Art, can I walk you home today?'

'I don't see why not. Probably won't be anyone at the house, and I'd appreciate the company.' At this, he gave me a little smile, and my efforts felt justified. So after the last bell rang, I met him at the flagpole in front of the school, and we set off.

Our town was a small one, on the outskirts of Baltimore proper. Never could I have guessed how far this young child walked every day to go to school, especially in the unyielding weather which always permeated our region. We walked west, first on a sidewalk, until that ended. Then we took a dirt road, covered in snow, until it hit a major boulevard. I choked several times on the smog from passing cars, but Art seemed unfazed; he stared forward with the determination of Odysseus, another favorite of mine.

We walked along that for what must have been twenty minutes. Art kicked rocks and loose pieces of asphalt the whole way. There was little conversation, and what little conversation existed was not substantive and revealed little about his home life, which I continued to grow more curious about.

We pulled up to a small rest stop on a forested road. A sign read: warm apple cider; five cents. I suggested we stop, given that the weather had penetrated my gloves and my feet were getting tired, but Art refused, citing that he lacked even a penny on his person. Ma and pa, he said, didn't trust him with their money; he was too young and would spend injudiciously. I grew frustrated as I began to regret the trip and remembering that, somehow, I had to get back to my own house to cook Magpie dinner.

Before I knew it, we were in a new town. We had traversed fields, walked briefly through a forest on what appeared to be a deer trail, and crossed a stream; my shoes were caked with mud from across the state, and my socks were soaked through. We popped out onto a narrow road from a dense growth.

'Art, how far until your house.' I think he could begin to tell I was frustrated.

'It's just up here.' This confused me, as we were on a road surrounded by trees as far as the eye could see. Across the parkway, another small snowed-in path appeared, and after no more than ten seconds of walking on the path, I could see what Art called his house.

Though a house it likely once was, given its frame, to

deem it as such now would be inaccurate. But, with the utmost composure, Art walked up to the front, kicked in the door, and walked inside. I, however, stood outside in the snowy forest for a minute, trying to fathom the journey I had just undertaken and its reward, or lack thereof.

There were two wooden pillars which supported a balcony jutting out from the second floor, but the left pillar had snapped, and the balcony fell with it, as if suspended only by a piece of fishing line. Behind each pillar was a window, but each of the four panes was smashed in, either by a projectile or by time. The front door was framed with white wood, but the top board hung cockeyed. A cross with a figurine of Christ hung on the wall, but it seemed almost broken and cracked.

Only the nonchalant way little Art entered the house gave me the courage necessary to take a large step over the snapped stair onto the front porch. Crumbled chairs sat on the ground to my sides. The door was ajar from when Art had entered. I pushed it open and took my first steps inside. I saw his school bag tossed to the side of the room.

The interior was quite simple. To my left a sitting room, and to my right a dining room. Dividing them was a staircase. Behind the dining room, which I could see because there was no wall, was a filthy kitchen, and behind the sitting room was a pile of rubbish, which I assumed was once a part of the sitting room. It appeared there was a bathroom in the corner of it all.

The eerie silence on the lower level led me to believe that Art had gone upstairs, perhaps to change clothes, if he had such things. So I took the liberty of seeing myself around. I walked in a counterclockwise direction, starting my tour in the dining room. Like the rest of the house, one of the table's legs had splintered, and chairs lay sprawled on their backs, littering the ground. Interestingly, there was relatively nice china on a nearby table, but years of dust and grime had collected on it, and I did my best to stay away. Each of the plates which sat the table had a different bird on it; my father had taught me some, so I recognized the black bird, the blue bird, the cardinal, and the crane, among others.

In the kitchen spoiled vegetables sat on the counter. I pulled up my coat to mask the stench. A broken cutting board parked itself on the counter. The grout around it had turned black from years of neglect. But on the cutting board was a half-chopped eggplant. Half of it was sliced, and the other half rested like a Christmas ham. The knife used to chop it was nowhere to be seen. I glanced up and saw the peeling ceiling. Flakes of it floated to the ground like the snow outside the walls, and a perpetual haze sat in the room. It stung my nose like a bee.

The pile of junk was truly that, junk. But the sitting room possessed all manner of fascinating objects. It was the only room I had seen which bore some semblance to its equivalent in a regular house. There were plush red chairs and a long blue sofa. None of the furniture matched, but given the state of the rest of the house, I thought that a non-issue. I sat down in one of the chairs, the one with less dust and cobwebs. There was some art on the walls, but nothing too sophisticated.

There was a picture of a pinecone, picture of a pine tree, and picture of a cedar tree. These I knew. There were more I didn't, but most all the paintings or pictures were of some small nook of nature. The glass cover on several of the images had been smashed, and several of the frames had decayed.

The mantle held a variety of small pictures. Some of them depicted a baby, whom I assumed was Art, and some showed a family. The dirt and grime on the family pictures made it challenging to discern the pictured people's countenances. But as far as I could tell, they appeared as happy a family as any.

# VII

## DIARY OF HANNAH HERRMAN

*January 20th (cont'd)*—But as I sat in the parlor, I began to notice some of the finer, more gruesome details the room had to offer. Little patches in the pinstriped wallpaper looked as if pepper had been shaken onto the wall, and opposite that was a broken window, which, it appeared, was shattered by more than a rock. There were slits in the wallpaper, as if the walls had been stabbed many times, and quite violently. There was even a large gash, around which the paper peeled away and the wood beneath became was exposed. My concerns were affirmed when I noticed small red streaks, of what I immediately concluded was dried blood everywhere: on the stairs, on the banister, on the sofa, on the walls, on the paintings, and on the pictures. Family pictures with blood caked on them, I thought. Now how does that come to be? I was uneasy. The place was a dump and, by my observations, a scene of horror.

I was taking it all in when Art called my name from the

stairs. I was so vulnerable in the moment that even hearing my name made me jump and pray that I made it out alive.

'Yes, little Art, is everything okay?'

'Certainly, but I think it's time for you to go. The Father is coming by soon, and he does not like it when there are others here.' Just the notion of one dubbed the 'The Father' sent chills down my spine. 'He comes when the sun hits the road, so it's almost time.' Little Art seemed confident and composed enough that I did not worry for him, however much I should have; I was partly consumed by worry for myself and my own wellbeing.

'Little Art, I don't suppose that you have a telephone somewhere around here?'

'Not around here, but there's a resting stop a quarter mile down, and they have a telephone that works sometimes.'

'Well, okay then. You take care of yourself. Make the whoever this father is does not do anything bad to you.'

'Hannah, he swept away my offenses like a cloud, my sins like the morning mist, and he has returned to me, for he has redeemed me.' This sounded oddly familiar, like a biblical wisdom, twisted for some cynical purpose. I walked up to him to say goodbye, and maybe to give him a hug. But as I approached him, smells seeped down from the second level, and formed a wall around the little boy. It could only be described by rotting fish, rotting vegetables, and rotting eggs all in one. Without much more commentary from either of us, I made my way to the door.

'I'll see you tomorrow, little Art?'

'I don't see why not,' he said, grinning.

I turned left out of the snowy, wooded path. After a few minutes of walking, I turned to look west at the setting sun behind me. The trees framed it beautifully. But emerging from a mirage came a rickety-old Tin Lizzie. It stumbled down the road until it got to the snowy path which led to Art's house. The driver's door opened, but it formed a wall with the car on one end and the forest on the other, so I could not clearly make out the figure who dashed towards the house behind it. I would be lying if I said that I was not concerned at least a hair for little Art.

In the whole process, I had almost neglected my own safety. It was dangerous for a black girl to be out by herself, especially after the sun set and the light of day was no longer a partial shield. So, always conscious of my surroundings, I made my way to the rest stop where it was one of those days the phone was working. I dialed my home phone—which we had just recently gotten for the holidays; it was very exciting.

But while I waited for my mother to arrive in her dinky car of make and model unknown to modern men, I saw a tragedy that has forever left a mark in my mind. I stood outside the parking lot and gas area. I was slouched against the tree; the alternative was sitting in front of a gas pump, and I decided I would walk the extra hundred yards for the fresh air. The breeze blew through my hair, and the air flowed through my nose and mouth. There was a black man filling up his car with gasoline some hundred yards away on the other end of the parking lot. The gas machines were lined up in a line, and there was six of them. This, I think, was a lot. They were all a nice crimson red.

I heard a grumbling noise come from the creek I had just walked over; from the West, I assumed. An old truck sped towards the rest stop. When it reached the rest stop, I expected it to continue down the highway, given its speed. But much to my surprise, the front wheels twisted and the truck slid into the parking lot, grazing the concrete pylons to its side. The breaks screeched and the cab of the truck pressed hard on the two front wheels—as if the back wheels were about to be lifted into the air. The truck was old and dusty. Canvas wrapped the back like wrapping paper. It was similar to those trucks which carried the men to the factories early in the winter mornings. The windshield was so dirty I could not make out the driver. When it stopped, the cab doors swung open with feverish intensity. Whoever is in there, I thought, must be awfully mad.

Two thug-looking white men emerged from the cab, one from each side. They wore white buttoned shirts, and their shoes were worn and tattered. Another man in similar dress emerged from the rear compartment. Together, they looked as threatening a group as I had ever seen. Their brows were furrowed, and their cheeks were red. Their lips were pursed with anger, and there was a slight tilt to their heads. I ducked behind the tree I was leaning against; like mother had taught me, can't get hurt if no one sees you coming.

The three men approached the man getting gas. They surrounded him like a pack of wolves encircling its prey. The men getting gas put his hands to his face. And not another moment passed before the fattest of the three had swung a punch and the man getting gas dropped to the ground.

What I proceeded to watch was the ultimate villainy of man. The three white men who had emerged from the truck pummeled the man getting gas. They kicked and yelled and punched and grabbed. Tears collected in my eyes, and my heart began to beat like a hummingbird's wings. I could not make out what they were saying. But from the flashes of red, I could tell the man getting gas was bleeding.

I turned my back to the fight, horrified by what I saw, still hidden behind the tree. I gripped the bark so tight that it began to peel away from the tree. Tears streamed down my cheeks, and I panted like a dog out in the sun. I just wanted it to be over. I just wanted it to be over. I just wanted it to be over.

But then, as I think back, I had anger too in my heart. A fire ignited within me. I peeked out from behind the tree— tears and heart and breathing and all—but my face was relaxed. Neither the anger nor the fear I felt could take hold of my body and limbs and actions. I stood there and watched—in horror and in fear.

So I returned to my hidden position as the violence continued. The shouting continued and the yelling continued. It all continued. For how long, though, I am not sure. Time became a figment of my imagination. I could have aged a several decades or jumped back in time by a century. The scene will stay in my mind forever.

I sat on the grass, now gripping it instead of the bark.

The grass was more gentle than the bark. It did not leave the same scratches and scars. It blew with the breeze while the bark was firm and unbending. It grew and died and grew and died. But the bark just stayed.

At last, I heard the familiar sounds and clanks of my mother's old Model T. I could not decide how to broach the subject of what I had just seen, so, for the time being, I kept the atrocious account to myself

But I did consent to tell her about Art. I thought maybe she should have some reaction to a white boy showing up at our colored school. He could be sitting in white classrooms with tiles on the floor and fancy projection machines. But instead he sat with us, in our wooden desks which creaked when you sat in them, and where the sound of chalk on the chalkboard never escaped the mind. I told her about my afternoon adventure, omitting, of course, the fight; she did not approve—I should not have expected her to.

She scorned me for being so foolish as to walk home with a white boy, all alone, and for going into a house with him, all alone. A tried to explain this was no ordinary white boy, and that his house and living situation was the most fascinating I had encountered. But her voice rose, and I receded into my shell. She dismissed my candor and continued driving, upset as can be.

When I got home, it was dark outside and Magpie asked if we could exchange tales again. I was still shaken by her story of the man and the angel, but was reluctant to deny her the opportunity to let her imagination run wild. I spent a few minutes around the house, washing my hands and cleaning the counter, before I gave in to her cunning. She smiled, and knew she had won. So we curled up on the couch with warm milk under as many blankets as we could find. The curls in her hair rested again my chest and she looked at me like a child stares at the stars. She rest her head against my chest and began:

Once upon a time, there was a woman. Her family lived in a large house in a cedar forest made from cedar wood. She was so beautiful that every day, many, many men made a long journey through the forest to ask her to marry them. They offered her cows and sheep and pigs and more money than the mind could fathom.

But the woman did not like any of the men. They were attracted to her not because of her keen intellect but because of her beauty. So the woman devised a plan to take revenge on all the men who had asked to marry her.

At noon on the beginning of each week, she accepted a man's proposal and took his cows and sheep and pigs and money. Then, they would lie and sleep for six nights.

The first man came, and he offered her fertility, but on the morning of the seventh day, the woman inflicted a great and lasting pain on the man. He was bound by her curse to wail from pain for days and days and days without end.

The second man came and was a pilot, which was practically unheard of. He had little to give the woman, except his tales of heroism and bravery. So on the morning of the seventh day, the woman prayed and a strong bolt of lightning shot down from the heavens and set his plane ablaze. His vanity bound him to the earth forever, and he cried without end.

The third man came. He was boastful and too confident in himself. So on the seventh morning, the woman dug seven graves for him, and threw part of him into each, so that he could never truly rest in peace as one.

The fourth man came. He was a soldier, and a good one at that. So the woman lashed him for the pain he inflicted on others and cast a curse so any water to touch his lips should immediately turn to mud.

The fifth man came. He was a commander in the military. So on the last night as the man lay sleeping, the woman stole his uniform and replaced it with that of the enemy. And when the man wandered back to his encampment, he met a most gruesome end as his battalion peppered the apparent traitor with their fire.

The sixth, and final, man came. He was a lowly farmer, and for a moment the woman almost thought he approached her out of love. But he offered her his harvest, citing that her own food was rotted by evil from the men she had cursed and killed. This idea infuriated the woman and turned the man into a rat, forever bound to nibble the crops he had once grown.

One day, the woman was wandering through the cedar forest when she saw a hero, tall and chivalrous, from whom vanity had been vanquished. She loved him so dearly that she asked him to marry her. But the man had heard tales of the woman's treachery and declined her proposal.

Infuriated, the woman went to her father and together,

they vowed to seek revenge. But the father never got his revenge, and tears poured down the woman's cheeks for several years after. She was bound never to have a lover again.

The end.


Oh, Magpie.


## DIARY OF HANNAH HERRMAN


*January 21st*—When I got to school today, I was not sure exactly whom to approach about what I saw at the rest stop yesterday. It was quite awkward. I felt simultaneously brand new to the school and as if I knew every nook and cranny of it. When I walked into the courtyard before the big school doors, I stood in the middle of the action. I was isolated, and everyone's wandering eyes seemed to find their way to me. Even novel things, like going to the bathroom and finding a drink of water, became burdensome tasks. The fight weighed on my soul. I, however, am not one to let such a weight sit.

During the morning period, I spent most of my time gazing out of the window, thinking of what should be done; who, I wondered, could bear such a horrific truth? So I decided to let my best friend, Clementine, in on my secret, which at this point it felt like I was guarding. I approached her during the mid-day break: 'Clementine, can I talk to you about something that has been weighing on my soul real heavy?' So the two of us walked into the writing room, and under the eyes of all the papers we had published for a great number of years, I told her my story.

I told her all the gruesome details, and I omitted nothing. Afterwards it looked like a mule had kicked her straight in the gut.

# VIII

LETTER FROM CLEMENTINE SMITH TO HER
DAUGHTER
1945

Dearest Daughter,

I write to you now on my death bed to recount to you a story which has been suspended in my mind since it passed by my eyes. But there are, in this story, many other stories. There is the story of what Hannah saw. There is the story which Hannah told me. There is the story which I tell you. And, perhaps most significant of all, there is the story of how Hannah confronted the world—how she made it stare inward at its twisted heart.

I realize it is all very confusing, but I hope in my final hours that I can put to paper the truths of life as we know it, so that others may follow in Hannah's footsteps, and do what is right over that which is easy.

Hannah was a wild spirit in her youth, but the day that

she spoke to me about the brutal beating of Billy Herald, she was all but wild. In fact, she was quite calm. Only later did I learn that she was not without emotion. Instead, she had such extreme emotions which countered one other such that it only appeared she had no emotion at all.

At the time neither of us knew Billy's name, nor did we understand the motivations of the attackers, nor did we truly understand why what had happened happened. We were naïve, and we were young.

The truths of this world had not fully penetrated our minds, but the process was surely hastened by what Hannah saw, and the vivid way in which she relayed her account to me. You may not know this, but at the time Hannah was the editor of our dear Peter's Post, and the choices she made, both the Thursday after she told the story and some months after that, were I think, the right ones. They were not the easy choices, but the right choices.

She came to me during the lunch break. She looked beautiful as always. Sun rays bounced off of her sleek hair, which swayed back and forth with her steps. She was wearing overalls that day, which were quite dirty, caked in mud and such. This was not uncharacteristic of her.

Together, we went into the writing room, and she recounted the tale of what she witnessed. It knocked the wind out of me. And for several minutes, we sat there; we were both angry and sad. It was unlike anything I had ever known. We sat in each other's embrace, and we talked and talked and talked until the bells split us up. But before we parted ways, I spoke one last line: 'We need to tell the world of this. We need to do everything in our power so that something like this never happens again. Clementine, if this is reality, then we cannot hide it. We need to shine a light on it—we need to!' She took one more breath and looked at the wall of all the papers we had printed. And with that, she walked away.

I only saw her in passing for the rest of that day. There was more speed and purpose in her steps than I had ever seen before, and I had known Hannah since the first grade.

Admittedly I was scared. I knew from body language and the direction in which she looked when she spoke of her aspirations that she wanted to write about the Billy Herald in the paper. I was scared because I did not want to lose what little we had. Based on her account, only she had witnessed the beating, so there were no sources and her own recollection, from a journalistic perspective, was quite unreliable.

Believe me, daughter, I was on her side. I wanted to oust these bastards for the manifestations of evil they were. But I wanted to also make sure that Peter's Post would be able to print papers the next week, and the week after that, and the week after that. After all, we had just gotten our new machine with what little money we had scraped together from the town.

It was unfortunate, but my thoughts were valid. I was ardently against pursuing the men who hurt Billy Herald. Also recall, at the time, we did not even know who Billy Herald was. We were perplexed and confused. Hannah had one vision, and I had another.

The many stories I previously enumerated were made

more complicated by Arthur Lawrence's arrival the day of the attack on Billy Herald, the day before Hannah told me the story. He was a small white boy at a colored school. Hannah had some strange fascination with him, but the rest of us kept our distances. None of us could begin to fathom why he was there, why, in a time where he could have so much more at no cost, he chose to associate with us. Some of us were almost angered by it. Regardless, he complicated things—immensely.

But come Thursday, I was able to persuade Hannah to not pursue the story about a man whose name we did not even know. She was reluctant, but in hindsight, it was the right choice. We would have greater battles to fight in the coming weeks, with greater foes who were better armored.

She did not stop her quest for justice easily, though. There was much yelling, and so much passion. I admired that in her. She was hell-bent on achieving justice. I was beginning to think that what she witnessed had affected her internally, and that she was troubled coping with the reality she had to face. She may have thought that a weight had been lifted from her shoulders, but she looked far from it. She ceased combing her hair that week, and she arrived at school in the same pair of overalls every day. She became progressively more discombobulated and dissatisfied. It seemed like every waking moment, she was trying to convince us that running the story would benefit us all. I tried and tried to convince her that was far from the truth, and that, in its current state, we could not give the story the justice it deserved.

When, on Thursday, we finally made the decision not

to put the story in—despite that fact Hannah had written some ten drafts of it—she shrunk into her shell. Though it seemed like none of us had seen her for the entire week, it was the first weekend in years, it would seem, that we did not meet in the morning and play in the snow and make angels. Instead, she shunned us all. And to my knowledge, she spent that whole week and perhaps that weekend with Art. Normally I was able to tell what was going through her mind by looking deep into her eyes and watching the way her eyebrows twitched when I spoke, but now she was an odd one, plain and simple.

## DIARY OF HANNAH HERRMAN
### 1902

January 24th—For the whole week, I had walked home with Art after school every day, and from there, my mother picked me up at the gas station, scolded me, and made me promise that I would not do something so foolish again. But I kept doing so. One could say I was almost addicted to it. To every day experience the squalor in which he lived had me sympathizing for him.

But when I uncovered the nature of how his loneliness came to be, I could not decide on a single emotion, so I told no one. My brain was buzzing with emotions and was constantly retelling itself the story. The way by which he acquired his solitary life challenged every value ever instilled in me. I could not decide if it was moral, or if it was right, or if Art should never be able to see the light of day again, or even if I should look past it all for the good the little boy who found himself at the center of a very, very unfortunate situation.

And to think that it came to light not more than a few hours ago.

After school, we took our normal walk through town, across the fields, through the forest, and along the road. We got to Art's house around five and, since he was trying to be a hospitable child (having realized he would be having company more often), he tried to clean the kitchen as much as one could so that he could steep some tea, or coffee, or make some cheap dish. Still, I never saw a mother, or a father, or a grandmother, or an uncle—practically an invisible family. Every time I asked him, he would change the topic abruptly, tell me the sun was almost down and I best be going, or that his parents were simply away for a little while and would be home late that night, and leave early the next morning.

Tuesday, Wednesday, and Thursday, Art had taken the time to show me the upper rooms of the house. The stench I mentioned before had disappeared midway through the week, so I found the second level relatively hospitable.

It seemed marginally more livable than the lower part of the house. Art's bedroom, albeit ridiculously messy, was relatively collected compared to the rest of his house. He had drawings and books, as intelligent kids his age would; he even had a Bible. There was a bathroom, and although it reeked of feces and the toilet seat was caked in urine, the shower was comparatively clean, and it was clear that Art had used it.

But there was one room, located directly above the house's entrance, which Art would not let me into. I tried the knob, and it was locked. Sometimes, he said, he had the key, and sometimes, he said, he did not. But he would pull me away from the door, whether by words or actions, as to prevent me from further investigating. Naturally, I became quite interested in what was behind it. Every day I would poke, but Art would relentlessly refuse. Sometimes he would say The Father was coming soon and that I should immediately leave.

By Friday, I had grown accustomed to the rickety old house. I began to bring a large jacket so that when the cold winds easily penetrated the windows, I would not shiver. And I brought snacks so that I would not go hungry when all that was left in the kitchen was a half-cut eggplant. Sometimes I would ask Art what he ate, given that everything in the ice box was rotten or spoiled. Often, with a firm countenance, he would say: 'I get by. You don't need to worry.' And I did not. Over the few days I had known him, I began to respect him, as much as one could expect, and gave him his distance. Though he would never admit it, I was sure he enjoyed my presence as well. For Art, I think it was reassuring to know there was someone out there, in the big and scary world, that knew, even if I did not talk about it, the reality of his situation.

When I first went to his house, I believed his story about ma and pa and gram and uncle, and that grandma died and ma and pa were seeing her away. On Tuesday, Wednesday, and Thursday, I scratched at the surface and poked at the truth. And on Friday, reality exposed itself to me—it socked me the gut; it twisted my morals and strangled my values—that Art had murdered his own parents and lived an eternally lonesome life as punishment for his heinous crime. The story is so shocking, to recount it tugs up tears and claws at the chambers of my heart.

Upon arrival at the house, Art announced he was going upstairs to take a shower before he would come down and play cards as we had done several times in the week. He had been rolling around in the mud at school and was filthy from head to toe as a result. He threw his school bag to the side and ran up the stairs as fast as he could, tracking mud all throughout the house. When he turned the water on, I took the liberty of exploring the second level of the house more than I had been able to when Art was my guide; it was the first time I had been alone in the house without anyone to stop my exploration.

I first looked through his bedroom. Nothing out of the ordinary. Dirty laundry. Lots of dirty laundry—to be expected. The next room over was the study. Like the chairs in the dining room, this one was also knocked over. The square window above the desk was completely shattered, with no indication there had ever been a window there except the small shards that remained around the edges. On the desk was a stack of documents, from bills to taxes to magazines. Nothing that was of too much interest. There was a bookcase below the window. I could not recognize any of the titles, though some rang a bell. Like on the floor below, the walls in the study appeared as if someone had shaken pepper on them; it surely was odd.

The floor creaked and the door squeaked when I exited

the study. But the next room on my self-guided tour was the locked room, which I assumed was the largest bedroom in the house, since, assuming at that point the parents lived there, they had to sleep somewhere. I tried the door, but it was locked. I gripped it tighter, but it was still locked. I gripped it with two hands, but it was still locked. I gripped it with two hands and shook the knob with all the force I could muster—and it popped off. I did not quite know what to do, as I had not anticipated the opportunity to look into this particular room.

I stood there with the knob in hand, staring down at it. The sound of the running water continued behind me, and I smelled what in hindsight was iron. With the door unhinged, I took a deep breath and pushed open the master door.

There was a large king-sized bed, and the room was in perfect order, in stark contrast to the rest of the house. The wallpaper was grey with white stripes and the headboard, with the circular star window above it, was a cloudy white color. There were dressers to the side of the room, but all the clothes were neatly packed away, and all the drawers were tucked in. There was a chest with a mirror above it. The chest was open, and its contents were gone. Most interestingly, the mirror was shattered, but there was no glass to be found. The wood floor was clean with the exception of the little bit of dust which had accumulated on it in recent days, and the lavish Turkish rug which covered a majority of it was in near perfect condition. The tassels were straight and shot directly out from the carpet's edge.

Despite the fact the window had been blown out, it

was still dark in the room. Prevailing winds entered through the open slit in the wall and bounced off the bed, off the walls, off the dresser, and off the carpet.

Once I took in the various elements of the room, my attention turned to its center: the bed. On the bed lay two people, or, more accurately, the bloody silhouettes of two people. Though absent, they laid on the bed, as if still bound by matrimony. I could almost make out their arms reaching to clasp one other as death approached them faster than sound.

I stood in the room, paralyzed by fear for a full sixty seconds, though it seemed like an eternity. I still held the door knob in my hands. My mouth was open, and I fully realized were the smell came from. In the back of my head, I heard the running water shut off, so I quickly discarded the door knob to the side of the room, shut the door, and, as quietly as I could, tip-toed down the stairs the sitting room where I spent most of my time when I was in the house.

I pretended I was reading my book when Art came down the stairs as he was completely naked. I acted as if I did not notice, but he broke the silence and said: 'Don't worry, I just need to get a change of clothes from my pack.' So with my right hand, I blocked the image of Art bending over to retrieve his trousers.

Once he had put on his trousers, my eyes met his own. Though his curly black hair was often messy and full of dirt, the hot water had straightened it, the black threads hung to his shoulders like a veil around his stoic face. They were like little brown pebbles which could pierce any exterior. 'The door knob was missing from the bedroom door upstairs. I assume that you went in? You saw Satan and the Witch (and he sighed)? And you're probably scared, and confused, (he began to speak faster) and horrified and afraid and fearful and nervous and alarmed and worried?' He was depressed, yet pitiful, and all he said of me was true. I was all of those things simultaneously. I had never known such an emotion. But the people I saw laying on the bed was a jarring image. For all of the week, I knew in heart Art was secretive, but I had no idea the magnitude of his secret.

I was on the verge of tears. I had come to respect Art in some convoluted way—but I do not know if that was possible going forward if he was really the villain I saw before me. Whatever trust I had in him was thrown off a precipice several miles high: 'Art, I need you to just tell me what happened. Where are your parents? What happened to them? And why in God's name are those sheets bloodier than the Civil War?'

Art began to cry, just standing there. His arms were at this side, and he was not wearing a shirt. Tears dripped from his chin like the water that dripped from his long, black hair to the floor. His face turned red, and he began to shake. He cried and cried. He needed a parent, but they were evidently both gone.

But still he just stood there.

I began to fear for him. It was unlike anything I had ever seen before. He screamed and scurried up the stairs on all fours, tears still pouring down his face. I could hear him moan from my seat in the parlor. But when I looked up towards the source of the sound, I saw the planks that formed the ceiling bore dashes of blood which had soaked through from the room above. For five days now, I had sat in that chair, and never once recognized blood directly above me.

So I waited thirty minutes, just sitting there. I could not leave. Something kept me there in that seat in that house, though even now, looking back, I am not sure what it was. I was not afraid. I was not scared. I was at some equilibrium between the two, but I did not know what to do about it.

I walked up the stairs and into Art's room. No knock. He sat on his bed in the fetal position, his back perpendicular to the headboard. I sat on the floor, and our eyes met. He looked away. I tilted my head to try and catch a glimpse—nothing. So I sat there until, at last, he spoke. 'You know I didn't do it for no reason.' In the moment this statement sent chills down my spine, but looking back, it was warranted. 'They were awful, God awful. That's why I call them that: Satan and the Witch. They were that bad.' He snuffled and choked back another wave of sobs. I was still confused at the time. 'When I was born, I was born into heaven. This house was heaven on earth. But then it became less like heaven. And then heaven disappeared altogether. I know the Church teaches that heaven is a place, but I'm convinced that heaven—it's a state of mind and a way of life. I was born in this house, and I'll probably die here too. I just can never escape it, even when I try my hardest. The world is against me, and I've known it right from the start.' I watched tenderly as he spoke.

'When I was young, I had real parents. This house had

windows. And I ate real food. My ma and pa were nice. They were gentle. They worked hard but weren't educated. Granma would come over sometimes and teach me how to read. But it all went to hell. I'm telling you, I used up all my Lord-allotted goodness by age six. Pa was gunned down in front of me. Some gang thing. He was real into booze. I don't think the gunner saw me, but I sure saw him, and never forgot his face. And I saw him come back a few more times, and ma would to talk to him in the front yard. And eventually he came to stay. The man who killed pa slept in the same bed as my mother.

'That's why she's the Witch—because she did nothing to stop it. They would be touchin' each other in front of me in ways I didn't get. But she let it happen. She smiled, and sometimes she would start the touchin'. The bitch could have died the moment she first spoke with him, for all I cared. But her real crime was later. It started one night when I was sleeping in my bed and Haman came in. He had been eyeing me since he started staying, watching me as I entered the bathroom or read my books. I swear I had seen him, or some other figure, in the window when I took my bathes.

'He spoke in a soft and gentle voice, but I was half asleep and couldn't understand. I turned away from him, since light was coming in from the open door. I curled up tighter into a ball facing away from him. So I heard his steps walking away from me, and I felt at peace. I heard the door shut, and he left. But then I heard his steps again, and I was confused. I thought the door was shut and the light was gone. It took me a minute to realize that I was right. It struck me when I felt a figure curl up next to me in my bed. My eyes shot open and my heart began to beat faster. But the only thing I could hear was Haman whispering: ssshhhhh, don't want to wake your ma. He reached over me and placed his calloused hand on my stomach. He moved it in circles and I heard him exhale. The hot air from his breath touched my ears and made me recoil. Then he explored more and more. His exhales grew into groans, and I felt his other hand come to my front from between my side and mattress. And so then he had two hands on me, doing everything. Up and down, and side to side. Pinch and let go and push and pull. But I just laid there and did nothing. I just let it happen. And it happened that way for months. And then months turned into years. Every night, my hatred for him grew.' Art was crying again at this point: 'He perverted my heaven. He turned my life into hell. And for that, he is Satan. But Hannah, Satan touches us on earth, but he never really turns the final screw. He has despicable... minions do that for him—he has witches.' I was particularly interested in this, since I do not think that he had ever actually spoken my name.

'A few days before I met you, I was sick, vomiting in every direction. So the lights turned off. I waited an hour and Haman came into my room like clockwork. But in the middle of his ritual, I threw up all over the bed. He sat up and yelled at me, you fucker! and have some respect! I turned around to look at him, but what I saw in the corner of my room... (he grew silent) was the scariest thing that I had ever seen, scarier than seeing my father gunned down, scarier than being touched by Satan who did it, scarier than watching your grandmother die.

'It was ma. She was just standing there. And she was smiling. There was a palpable silence in the room. But she just stood there smiling. The women had lost all sense of reality. She stood there while Haman took advantage of me, and she enjoyed it. It was sick, Hannah. It was fucking sick! ...So the next morning, I found the gun that pa had hidden before he died, and I shot em'. They were both in the kitchen when I came down the stairs with the gun. When they saw it, ma dropped a mug and it shattered, and Haman started shoutin'. And I liked it like that. So I started shooting. My aim was stunk and took me a few shots to get used to the weight of the gun and the kick. But in those few shots, I chased them entirely around the lower level of the house. I shot at the windows and I shot at the walls and I shot at the dining room table and the sitting chairs. They ran up and barricaded themselves in their bedroom. But I was on a mission to vanquish evil from this house, and nothing would stop me. So with a few more shots I was through their pathetic plea of a barricade. And I stood above them. And I held the power. They were curled up in the bed like babies in a crib...

'Satan sat up in the bed and tried to talk—bang. And then there was the Witch. But in her last moment, she didn't cower like Satan. Instead, she began to laugh and said, Where did we go so wrong with you? With one last cynical smile, she looked up—bang—to a place she would never get to go. And so that's how I got here.'

I sat there struck by what I had just heard. But although I felt that I should have been afraid, sitting on the floor of a murderer's bedroom, with the killer some ten feet away, I was not—not in the slightest.

'But Art, who is The Father. He seems like the only person you have left.'

'His name is Father Marquise. He comes in the evening, sometimes. I went to Church to get over the sin of what I'd done, and he started coming over sometimes. Not regularly, but I am half sure he is a friend of Haman's, since he does the same nasty things.'

I spoke. 'Art, do you mean to say that a man of the church has been visiting you since you've been alone in this house doing the same vile things the man you call Haman or Satan or whoever did to you? A man of the church taking advantage of you in your pathetic state?'

He nodded. 'I could have killed him too. But he's not really a part of the Church. Pa taught me about the Church, and Father Marquise is nothing like Pa; I could call him Judas.' He smirked at that. Sometimes I underestimated Art; he was well-read.

'Art, why don't you— I don't mean to suggest that you should employ violence in any way... but...' I had spoken myself into a corner, and I could either recommend that he kill the man or take the abuse; both were nasty options.

'Hannah, I greatly appreciate all that you have done, and the time that we have spent together, but I need The Father on my side at all costs.' I could not understand less what he meant by this. I was perplexed beyond belief.

'I know it might be hard for you to think, Hannah, but

I have little left to hold onto in this life, and I want to live. Only the prospect of salvation keeps me here. And sure, The Father and his rituals aren't the most orthodox, but it's all I got left. No church in the right mind would take me in. The physical pains I take are earthly, but my soul can be saved!' He crawled off his bed and over to me. He put his hands on my knees. 'I still have a chance, and Father Marquise says he can do that for me, as long as I comply. The abuse I take is just payment for his troubles.'

'But Art, you killed your mother for the same crime?' I was at a loss for words.

'Yes. Yes. Yes I did. And I can't take that back. But can't you see? That's exactly why I need Father Marquise—it's because I've sinned. He and his idolatrous ways are my only ticket off this rock. And Hannah, I need that ticket.'

# IX

LETTER FROM CLEMENTINE SMITH TO HER
DAUGHTER
1945

It came time to return to school, but Hannah was more
secluded. She was not her normal, gregarious self. She had been
social and eager to hear about your day and your morning,
but now she was cold. She stayed to herself. When I would
approach her, she would walk away. That Monday was the
lowest point of our friendship. She refused to look at me, let
alone speak with me. I tried to be social with her, but all my
attempts were futile.

And when it came time for lunch, I searched the
courtyard high and low for Hannah. I looked behind all the
normal trees, but could not find her. So I turned my search
inward. Students typically were not allowed in the school
building during lunch times except when it was during rain
or snow. I snuck in a side door and tip-toed down a corridor.

I stopped just short of the writing room, and could hear footsteps. Sure enough, it was the cadence of Hannah's walk. It was very distinct—though, I am of the mind that if you listen to anyone walk for long enough, you will think their cadence is unique when, in fact, millions do the same.

I walked in and Hannah was pacing back and forth. But unlike the cold facade she had shown me in the courtyard, her face was excited with rage and determination; the only time I had seen her in a similar state was when she pursued the story on Billy Herald. It took me only a few seconds to become concerned.

'Clem, I have got it. I know what story will really put Peter's Post on the map. It's nasty, and it's vile. But people will eat it up. They will be scared. They will be angry!' I nodded my head to encourage her to continue. 'I found out, but I cannot tell you how, that there is a priest at a local— well I guess it's a cult— who is touching kids.'

At this, I sighed. For the story, we would either need to persuade the priest to tell us his story, or convince a handful of kids to tell us their stories. I could not discern which party would be less willing. So for the rest of the lunch, we sat together in the writing room, just as we had done the day after the attack on Billy Herald.

I could tell she was hiding something having to do with Art. His name came up too many times in our conversation for my own comfort. At last, I coaxed it out of her—the full story, in all its unabashed sadistic and horrifying glory. I was mortified. But I, too, began to feel as though there was perhaps material to this story.

Together, we elected to maintain secrecy with regard to it for the time being. Only if we collected enough evidence and talked to enough people could we write a substantive report on Father Marquise.

It did cross my mind that both Hannah and I were parishioners, though not of his denomination. Our town had its own local church with a reverend, and everyone adored him. In the parish we sang and prayed and did all manner of holy things, which most of the town truly enjoyed. We were all better off because of it.

In Baltimore proper... their parishes often confused me. Their priorities were out of line, and their faculty were doubtable. It was ironic that even in our run-down little town, we were closer to God than anyone in the big city of Baltimore. Those other parishes, like the one Father Marquise ran, and Art attended, put all these people and rituals between them and God. I sure didn't understand.

Together, Hannah and I devised a plan. We would become sleuths and survey our prey like eagles; we would infiltrate his lair. Sure, it might have been reckless, but we were excited by the prospect of discovering something great—or, for that matter, horrible. We put our plan into action the following week. Together, we would go to the group which Father Marquise led, and we would find the bastard. Somehow we would collect evidence—we had not thought that part through yet, but we were determined.

So came Sunday morning, when Father Marquise's

church met, according to Art. They were not good Christians, but instead thought they were. Hannah had learned to drive recently, so she lied to her mother that we were going to attend a ceremony of some sort and do some good, old-fashioned reporting. Hannah's mother had always been real supportive of Peter's Post, so long as it did not involve us getting involved with people of a different color. Naturally, we assumed, she would be quite averse to our plan as it was, so it was a fairly logical step for us to concoct this lie. It was small but necessary.

We drove in the little car for quite a while, picked up Art from his run-down excuse for a house, and arrived at the church (for lack of a better word, since the building undoubtedly should not be called a church) to which he had directed us thirty minutes before the service was set to begin. Though the church was not all too far from us, the winding road took us up through the hills which functionally served as a barrier between the town and the real city of Baltimore, with the factories and people and such. And for the most part, it served its job. The white folk seldom came to the town, and we seldom crossed the hill, with the key exception of the men going to work in the wintertime.

The church was a big building, though neglected in its old age. It was perched on the top of a hill. We could look out from the steps in front of it and see our little town, half on a hill, half not, in the distance. In the early Sunday sun, the roofs and the cross reflected light back at us, and the valley in between the two hills gleamed like a stream. There was life teeming within it, but only when one looked closely could they see it.

Though this part of the city was quite white, we found that it was more a working type—less of the industry big-shots, more of the working low-life. They were the drunks and crazies of the city, but they all came together well on Sunday mornings in their Sunday best; though, I think Hannah and I were dressed better than the lot of them. Though we wore simple clothes, far from the ornate garb of the few wealthy who attended the parish, our clothes were indicative of who we were at the time: simple, young, and eager. Even Art, in the 'nice' clothes he could muster, looked presentable.

Art was reluctant to bring us that morning. Hannah had explained to me the complicated relationship between Art and the church. It took me aback, but I had learned by then not to question the odd human who is Arthur Lawrence.

At this time, Hannah and I were still relatively unsure of our plan. We had discussed it in brief, but our conversation lacked specifics. Our current plan involved watching The Father closely to notice how he interacted with the children of the group. We did not have the luxury of capturing images as we have now, so we were forced to find children to interview. But to interview children would be to reveal to their parents that their beloved father (and from what Art told us, he was beloved) was abusing their children in ways any god would not approve of. We stood by the car admiring the day and watched the people walk by and watch us. There was a certain daze in their eyes; they were hunched over slightly and tired, susceptible to forceful speech of conviction.

We stood on the edge of the parking lot overlooking the valley. Behind us, we heard the church doors swing open, and Father Marquise stepped out of the building. He did not venture far—remaining on the covered deck immediately outside the church—but his presence was intimidating. The sun rendered his glasses completely white and hid his eyes. He wore a long robe of a green material. He was some fifty yards away from us, but it felt as if he were standing beside us. He gave Art a nod, who returned the gesture. When he looked at Hannah and I, he tilted his head and introduced a furrow to his brow. He was disappointed that two colored girls were attending his service; no question about that.

I snatched Hannah's hand and returned our gaze to the snowy valley in front of us. Even though I had looked away, I could tell The Father kept his eyes trained on us. For him, after all, we were the impurity of his art.

Art kept to himself most of that morning. He was the quiet type, no question. Most of the cues we got from him so as to fit in with the Catholic parishioners stemmed from a nod in a particular direction or a one-word command: 'Left, right, yes, no...' things to that effect.

It eventually came time for us to enter the building. And it is at this moment that I felt the eyes of a city fall upon me. I felt naked when I entered the vestibule, as one man turned, then a woman, then a family, and before I knew it, everyone was staring. The phenomenon was only momentary. Art eventually picked up on what was happening and directed us inwards. We repeated after Art as he crossed himself from some water in this funny little bowl at the entrance of the church, and then followed him to the nearest open pew, which was evidently towards the back of the room.

Until then, I operated under the mindset that were in a brackish area of town, someplace of geographic transition, from the colored population of the more rural area to the white population of the industrial city.

But I could not have been more wrong.

I was stranded on an island. Hannah was on a nearby island, and Art was off on a raft in the boons. But I was stranded nonetheless. We may have been the love of the town back at home, but here we were made outcasts by no fault of our own. It was a disease of the mind, I tell you.

Father Marquis entered with his assistant and took his place at the front of the congregation. For the next twenty minutes, Hannah and I followed along with Art as he stood up and sat down, and moved our mouths as he and the other attendees spoke back to the priest in a language I certainly didn't know.

At last, Father Marquis began his sermon, which I guess the Catholics call a homily. Luckily for us, he did this part in English. And he was an eloquent speaker. I have no problem seeing how persuasive a man he is. His voice is alluring, like a siren, and his smile is like a snare. How many, I wondered, had fallen for his devilish trap? The Father spoke:

'Today, my friends, we examined the story of David and Goliath. It is a tale of a true underdog, wherein victory was only achieved with the aid and will of God. In our lives, we all face giants. They are powerful and intimidating, and their armor may be impenetrable, but when we invest our faith in God, anything is possible.

'Goliath embodied the power of the Philistines. Their might was unfettered, and the future of the kingdom of Israel hung in the balance. Perched on either side of the valley, neither army would descend towards the other, fearing a strategic blunder. So, the Philistines employed the ancient tactic of one man versus another. In doing so, they hoped to avoid the bloodshed and carnage promised by a clash of the armies.

'And even King Saul was scared of Goliath, stricken with fear and cowardice. The question must be posed: should we let our fear of giants determine our actions, or should we let our faith determine our fate against all odds? Think my friends, think.

'When David stands before Goliath, though, he is not intimidated. He sees a man who defies the will of God and will consequently lose their duel. He is confident and unafraid. Only the power of the Lord will save the lowly shepherd with his lowly sling and its lowly stones. To the objective observer, David is disadvantaged in all ways. His weaponry is inferior and he lacks armor. Goliath though, is overconfident—plagued by hubris. And the Lord frowns upon this.

'So, my dear parishioners, what lessons do we learn from this tale? First, we must be faithful, both to God and ourselves. We must trust the Lord is there, watching over us. He guides us like he guided David's stone to Goliath's brow—his Achilles' heel. Goliath dwarfed David, but because David had faith, placed his trust in the Lord, and stayed true to himself in his faith, the Lord saw him though his troubles. The second lesson we must learn is that we must, sometimes blindly, place our faith in the Lord. As David walked into the valley, he did not know what the outcome of the duel would be. He only knew that he could put himself out, and that the Lord might save him in return. The third and final lesson is that we must not fear giants when we have the Lord watching over us. We must be unfazed by a giant's speech and unaffected by a giant's confidence. So long as the Lord is on our side, we are safe in our faith.'

It was a perfectly fine sermon, not unlike things which I had heard before. David this... Goliath that... It was all too typical of these types of things. There was a particular audience for things much more complicated. The crowd, this morning, was not one of scholars and theologians. It was the workers of the city, and they did not attend church for metaphysical advice. They gathered on Sunday mornings for practical advice in life, and to be seduced by a voice that tells them their worth. They were competent enough to apply the David and Goliath metaphor to elements of their life, whether their giant was a factory or a boss. And more often than not, these people inserted themselves as the David figure.

But I felt they were all Goliath.

# X

## DIARY OF HANNAH HERRMAN

*January 29th*—The twists and turns of a single day never cease to amaze me. Clem, Art, and I began our morning at the church on the hill across from the town. The speech, or reading (I'm not sure what the correct term is for heathens), was not of particular interest, nor was it among the better sermons I have heard. The speaking of our own parish's Reverend John are more insightful and inward-looking by tenfold. What did speak to me this morning, however, were children, five of them to be exact. Each with a story more horrifying than the last, though none so gruesome as the tale of our own Art.

After the sermon came to a halt and the people of the parish awoke from their slumber, the crowd rallied for their part in the show. Whereas Reverend John back at home blessed the bread and wine in English, Father Marquis reverted back to Latin and led the congregation through the Lord's Supper.

I don't think I was supposed to, but I went up there anyway.

I followed Art's lead, kneeling in front of the loathsome priest. Father Marquis stared not at me but scornfully at the color of my skin as he placed the host on my tongue.

'Corpus Domini Nostri Iesu Christi custodiat animam tuam in vitam aeternam, Amen.'

I had no particular idea what that meant, but it made my blood boil that such an evil man was participating in such a holy act. After the Eucharist, Father Marquis led the procession out of the church. Some, eager to leave, immediately set off for the doors. Others stayed behind to mingle with one another and, evidently, The Father, once he returned inside the church. Clem and I stood perched in the back, and Art set off for the car, not wanting any involvement in any plan that was about to unfold. Little did he know there was no plan… just a goal.

We stayed in the back long enough that the majority of the crowd had dissipated and moved on to the chores of their day. I assume some went to factories, and others returned to their homes to rest for the coming week. But Clem and I, we were like flies. We would bother until we got what we came for.

We waited for a little more than an hour. Several times, Art reentered the building wondering about when we would at last be out and ready to depart. Every time we said: 'Just a few more minutes.' At some point in our stay, the church organist began her practicing. Her hair was long and straight, and she was dressed in all black. But the frills… The music she played was sonorous, but none so much as Handel's "Sarabande," and once she began playing, the sarabande was the only piece she played until we departed. The dance was the only piece I recognized from our lessons at the church near the center of town, so perhaps for this reason it rang in my mind for so long. It was scary and, in reflection, the perfect backdrop for the events which were about to unfold.

'Clem, do you see that?' I think she had half dozed off given that we had sat in the same position for nearly an hour.

'What? What are you looking at?' At the other end of the building, The Father crossed in front of the altar and moved towards a wooden door on the side of the building. It was an oak rectangle with ornate baroque decorations. There was gold trimming along the top, green velvet curtains hung around it. Angels were engraved above the entrances. They had broad avian wings and long, flowing robes. Alongside them was the phrase: Fructu non foliis arborem aestima. I did not have the slightest clue as to what it meant, but, like the Sarabande, I could not get it out of my head. It was a worm of the mind.

'Now what do you suppose he is doing? All the people have left, but only now he is heading to the corner...' So we sat and waited a few more minutes. But it struck me: The Father had not noticed our presence despite the fact we sat out in the open. We were in plain view but were not of significance to him.

'Look over there!' Clem grabbed my shoulders and turned me towards the door. She spoke in a soft voice, but urgent nonetheless. The outside was bright, so at first I could only make out the silhouettes of a group of people entering the building—some small, some large. As they came into focus, I realized it was a family. I cannot say I was astonished. We were, after all, in a church. They came in together, one father, one mother, one daughter, and one son, and made their way over to the oak door.

'Clem, this is sickening to watch.'

'I know, Hannah, I know. But we need to do it if we're to show the world this monster.' So we watched patiently as the mother entered, and then the father. Both parents came out in some degree of ecstasy, either trembling and mumbling, or flat out in tears. All the while, the children sat the wooden benches, amused by the pictures of angel flying above them. And then it came their turn—first, the girl.

She looked like a smaller version of her mother. They wore similar green dresses with plenty of frills and fluff. They plumed at the bottom like a flower hung upside down. Her shoes clicked and clacked on the wooden floor, like the sad sarabande. Time passed, and no noise came from behind the door, not that we would hear any if it did. The parents and brother sat, contented, on the wooden bench. We could, from our position, make out their faces. Together, they were here on a familial mission: to purpose; but in the process, they came down with a severe case of... Well I am not even sure what it is called. They appeared blind to The Father's malicious intent, and if they were, they certainly did little to show it. They were swept up by his words and his actions. He offered what they sought, and they took the bait.

So the boy went in and came out. I could not be too sure from where I sat, but his countenance appeared as obedient as the rest of the family's. So they left all together, but

The Father remained. Clem seized me, and we quietly made our way towards the exit of the church. 'We should get to the boy and girl before they leave, so we can see if they can tell us anything about what transpired in the box!' She again spoke in an urgent tone, though her voice was soft. We tip-toed our way to the exit. It was not particularly far, so we arrived before the family. But when Father Marquis looked up and saw Clem and I standing there, two colored girls blocking the exit of their white church, he wrapped his arms around his children as to protect them from some evil spirit descending upon them. Slowly, as if we were wild animals, he backed the family away from us and quickly ushered them towards a side door. 'Wait! We just want to help. Something nasty happened in that box— we know it!'

'You best stay away from this house of God. Stay in your backwater and don't come out. You need not forget the separate in separate but equal!' At once, a hurricane of emotions flooded into me. I was confused, angry, sad, and tormented simultaneously. And to think that when the man had entered, Clem and I felt sorry for him in some capacity, as we knew what was about to happen to his beloved children. But we were also flustered beyond belief. If we were chameleons, our skin would be a scarlet red. If we were an element, we would be fire. Our kindness was met only by callous and thoughtless rejection. We resumed our seats in the back of the church and fumed. The lightning and thunder in my soul was practically audible. But together, Clem and I sat in each other's embrace, and far overhead, the storm passed.

Time passed too. Another family came in, and another, and another after that. Four families came in, all of different composition with regard to sons and daughters and teens and infants. They left too. Each time Clem and I approached them as they tried to leave, they tarnished us in some way. Some ignored us completely, as if we were figments of their imagination and voices in their head. Some spat obscenities and cursed at us like in our first encounter. Others took a more caring approach (I write sarcastically) and acknowledged our presence but moved along their flocks with the same haste as those before.

The fifth family was different, but perhaps family was not the correct term. When they stumbled in, it was only a boy and his mother. My interest was piqued because, though the mother was white, the boy, who was no older than twelve, was clearly not the product of two white parents, nor two black parents. They took their turns in the booth. But this time, the mother went quickly. She was out before Clementine and I had finished a single round of our game of eye-spy in the religious paintings. The young boy, however, took ages. I had to spy numerous angels and crucifixes and devils before he finally emerged. But when he did, so unlike the other children. While the others emerged from the box as innocent as they entered, he was slouched and walked slowly. He and his mother made for the exit, and we approached. He remained hunched over, and drew his limbs inward. His eyes were large, and tears had accumulated. His jaw hung in limbo, as if there were words to be spoken, but no air to do so.

'Excuse me, ma'am.' She looked up at me with a kindness not present in any of the others whom we had approached.

'Yes, how can I help you?' Even in her inquisitiveness, she maintained a certain gentleness.

'My friend and I, we were just hoping to talk to your son about... his... (I stammered looking for the right word)...' Clem jumped in: 'Faith. About his faith.'

At this, she brought her child closer. But unlike the others, she did not so out of malice, but simply concern for her child, as any mother would.

'Well, I'm afraid that we actually need to be on our way.'

'No ma'am, please, this is very...' The urgency in my voice rose.

'No really, his father is waiting at home for him, and we best be on our...'

Clementine spoke: 'Son, is your father black?' She did so with the most bluntness and disregard for politeness, but it was refreshing. The boy looked to him mother, who sighed, and spoke on his behalf.

'Yes. But for his sake he does not come around here much anymore, and for your sakes, I most kindly recommend you do the same. Some of the others looked not too kindly on his regular attendance and worship with them. The only reason we still come is because Stone insists on seeing Father Marquis.' I thought 'Stone' was an unusual name for a child, but then I remembered that we often referred to my sister as

Magpie, so I thought little of it. So Clementine spoke to Stone.

'Stone, why do you come to see The Father? What is it about him that makes him so special that no other father can do for you?' She kept her voice down as to avoid detection by the vile man who still sat in the box. For all we knew, he could be eavesdropping on our every word.

'Well,' now the child spoke, 'he says that I have sinned, and in some ways I have. My mother and I talked about it, and he says that I sinned a lot, but my mother says not. But he says that I can only get to heaven and have salvation if I see him and confess my every sin.' His answer sounded rehearsed, and his mother's eyes sank to gaze at her shoes.

I understood later that going to a priest to talk about sin was a normal practice for Catholics, and that Father Marquis was just taking advantage of this alone time.

It sounded near the same as what Art told me; though when he spoke, he stressed the issue to the point of tears. Stone's mother let out a long sigh and gripped his hands tightly.

'Well, I think it's time for us...' She spoke, mustering the energy to leave the awkward conversation. Clem, in her bullish nature which I loved about her, cut her off abruptly.

'Stone, does he touch you? I mean does he make you feel a rat about yourself and what you've done and your place in God's world—and then grab you?'

Everyone's expressions changed as she spoke. My eyes widened. Though she voiced the real questions I wanted to ask, she did so with such confidence that I could hardly believe my ears. Stone's mother simply turned to look at him. Tears welled up in her eyes. It appeared that the final piece of a devastating puzzle had been found and put into its place to complete a most horrifying picture. She put her hands over her pursed lips, which were the only thing of color in her face; the rest had practically been drained of blood. More tears welled up. Then she moved her hands to her scalp. More tears—then her hands covered her eyes. Even more tears. It was still completely silent. Finally she embraced her child, who, all the while, had lost all expression in his face. And while his mother panicked, I faced Clementine and nodded a slow, disparaging nod.

So we quickly sat down Stone and his mother in the back of the church and conducted our journalistic obligations. Our questions were brief, but Stone's story was long. For such a young boy, he had a remarkably long story to tell. I have not the time nor space to delve into the all the subtleties and details, and though it was known all to his mother, it was just as remarkably awful as Art's story, or any that I had heard for that matter.

After they left the room. Clem and I sat back in our seats one last time. Having just filled a notebook to the brim with details, it was as if we had just come to the end of a long race, and while we knew there was still ample work to be done, we were relieved to have made it this far.

But as we stood up to leave, we heard the lock on the oak door click. The church was silent by then, and the click echoed throughout the room. From it emerged Father Marquis, adorned in the same robes. I had failed to notice how tall he was, but he was indeed a remarkably large figure. When stood fully erect, he stared directly at Clementine and me. From across the room, he spoke. But his voice was no longer that of a religious man; it was not warm, friendly, and inviting. It was voice of a criminal, cynical and disgusting as can be.

'Why do you come here? Do you not have birds and wild animals to tend to?' There was a long pause before he spoke again. 'I'd like to not see you here again. Every worshipper has his place in God's kingdom, but yours is not here.' As the towering figure came to silence, Clementine and I left without another word.

After we deposited Art at his residence, and he promised that The Father would not return in that day, we made one last stop: our own beloved church of color in the center of town, to speak with Reverend John. Perhaps, we thought, he could give us some guidance, as we were overwhelmed by both all we had learned and the task ahead.

# XI

## DIARY OF HANNAH HERRMAN

*January 29th (cont'd)*—Clementine and I arrived at Reverend John's parish in the mid-afternoon, and when we left, our exit of the church was greeted by the setting sun. It was the universe waving farewell to us for a good day's work. But before I spoke with the Reverend, I did not feel as if I had done a good day's work. In speaking with him, nothing physical changed. But my perspective was eternally shifted. I informed him of the day's actions with all details, but it is worth noting that I did not inform him on the subject of Father Marquis's sermon. Here are, as best as I can recall, the words which Reverend John spoke to Clementine and I, which have given my actions new purpose and renewed my love for the truth and resilience:

Have you heard the story of David and Goliath? Most people in the world, both religious and not, will tell it the story of an unlikely victory, a tale of faith, and a story to teach reliance on the Lord. And these things are true... to some degree... maybe. But there is much that is overlooked in this telling of the age-old tale. And it is easy to miss that which lies directly in front you, on the page as a matter of fact, because of the thoughts of the general populous which conflate your reading and interpretation. So let us start from the very beginning.

The story takes place in a valley where the two armies, the Israelites and the Philistines, are dug in on opposing ridges. The Philistines sought to invade the mountains, so the Israelites descended to defend their cities. They see one another very clearly, and there is no question in the others' presence. But neither side agrees to enter the valley first, for they both know that doing so would mean certain death for their army. They stand at deadlock.

To avoid bloodshed, the Philistines sent their strongest warrior down to the valley floor. His name was Goliath. He was tall as one could ever be and rose above the rest of the men. But in this reading, you have already missed a key element of the plot. Goliath is led down to the valley floor. He cannot make his way on his own. But I digress...

When David approaches King Saul, the King insists that David wear armor. In Saul's mind, this is David's only hope of defeating the giant. Without armor to protect him from Goliath's sword, he would surely perish. But the armor did not fit David, and David insisted that he should fight without it. Whether or not it is obvious, Saul made a mistake. He wrongly assumed that Goliath must be fought on Goliath's own terms.

But David was not a part of the infantry, and it would have been foolish for Saul to ask David to fight Goliath as an infantryman.

So with his five stones, David walked down, into the valley and approached Goliath. Goliath asks, 'Am I a dog, that you come at me with sticks?' This is of course, a foolish statement, because David only carries his shepherd's staff—just one stick. But Goliath sees multiple.

Our reverend paused for a while at this juncture.

So their duel begins, and David uses his sling and guides a stone to Goliath's brow which knocks him over. But, if you have not yet picked up on the theme of this telling, there is much you have overlooked.

Have you ever used a sling? I assume not, and neither have I. But I have been told by many wise men that a sling is not a weapon to be used lightly. It can hurl objects at startling speeds and to great distances with remarkable precision. And David had practiced his craft on the animals that attacked his herd of sheep. But my assumption is that you assumed the sling to be a flimsy weapon made by school children to fling pebbles at one another.

He chuckled to himself after saying this.

You assumed wrong!

He laughed even more, almost knocking himself over. It was a laughter from the gut.

Hannah and Clementine, dear children, think! Goliath was never going to win that fight! His vision was poor and he moved like a rock. His intelligence was lacking and the only thing which he had over David was his size. Even his sword could only reach an additional arm's length. David, however, was nimble and well versed in his use of a weapon which made it such that he would never need to get anywhere near Goliath! The sling is a powerful weapon, and David easily downed the giant.

Hannah and Clementine—find your sling, and in time all will be well.

With that he smiled and bid us good night. He retired to his chambers and that was the last we saw of him until the next Sunday. And we were left sitting on the wooden pews, staring at one another.

## LETTER FROM CLEMENTINE SMITH TO HER DAUGHTER

Reverend John's words were more or less the climax of the story. It was the point at which our minds and perspectives were forever shifted. We did not think much beyond that. Hannah and I placed our article at the top of Peter's Post that week. It elicited quite the reaction from the town. There was much ado about many things that week. And although Father Marquis was hardly ever seen in the town, and many people did not even know his name to begin with, the very idea of a priest touching kids made the town think.

Even more notable, though, was the greater city's reaction. Our piece got taken from us and printed in the city's journal. They did not run our names next to the story, nor did they say that it was from our dear Peter's Post—to deprive us of our work was the greatest injustice inflicted upon us yet.

Come summer, Art disappeared without a trace; I have a hunch that he told Hannah where he was going, as the two were always very close. But she refuses to admit that she knows, let alone that he told her. His life will go on, and I can only hope the best for him as much as I can hope the best for myself and my Hannah.

And at last, several weeks later, the bittersweet peach of victory came after all, when word looped back to us through all manner of hearsay that The Father had been removed from his post by the Pope in Rome. They sometimes talked bad about the Pope in our town and in the bigger newspapers, but it seemed to me that he did alright in this case. That night we ate chicken and beans. Our parents were not aware of our greater victory, though they were all too familiar with our local one. We ate well, not because our food was fattening or delightful, though the chicken was moist with flavor, but because our values had shot a stone so smoothly, so hard, so far, so precisely, that we knocked over a giant.

I am reluctant to say that I fear we did not cut off its head. In the grand scheme of things, we are still walking towards it to fetch the sword. But we had fought, and won, our little battle.

Daughter, be well in life. Know in light of the challenges you may inevitably face, that you are strong, and that despite with others think, you too have a sling. Find your stones, my child, and knock the giant to his knees.

With love from your mother,
Clem Smith

# XII

LOG OF ARTHUR LAWRENCE
Reflecting on June 13th–17th, 1927

*Evening of June 16th (reflecting on June 13th–16th)*—I joined the Union Pacific when it hit the Chicago Burlington near Cheyenne. I had just completed a job rounding up a group of destitute criminals near Buffalo. For months, they had terrorized the banks of northern Wyoming, west and east. In one week, they made the wild trip from Gillette, to Cody and back to Newcastle, where I inevitably apprehended them at gunpoint before law enforcement even had a chance.

They were a rambunctious and lethal group of vagabonds, but at the same time, they were as stupid as they were feisty. It was ultimately their downfall. One would imagine that such a wealthy and notable battalion of bandits would take a moment to check whether the exits of the building were cleared. With my pay in hand from the state government, I took the local line west out of Gillette, only to realize the peddler who had sold me the ticket forgot to mention that the tracks loop back around in southern Montana, and that if you really wanted to go west, you had to join the U.P. in Cheyenne. The farmers cannot tell their ups from their downs, let alone their easts from their wests.

With the spoils of my labor in hand, I took up in a rather spacious compartment in the sleeper car. I felt out of place, not because those around me possessed more wealth than I (with quite the wealth amassed through my work in recent years), but rather because of their lifestyles. So many of them had an arrogant countenance, while their servants and maids bore obsequious expressions. I detest that lifestyle. I live in the wind, and do so with swagger.

There was a most notable gentleman on the train, however, who used the on-board resources of a high-class individual, but hardly appeared as one. I did not see him often, because he had his own compartment in the same car as my own. But when I did lay my eyes on him, he did not speak. Instead, he stared out the window, as if contemplating his presence and purpose. He appeared lost in the labyrinth of his mind, taken and held hostage by his thoughts.

Several times I tried to approach him, but one of two things would happen. He would either fail to acknowledge my presence and continue to stare out the window, always the same window, from the same seat, or, he would look me dead in the eyes. It was all the more interesting when he did the latter, for I could look through his eyes and into the damaged core behind them. The way his face hung implied he had experienced hardship, and that it weighed on him greatly.

I suppose I was a bit cavalier in my approach to Marty Turner. I discovered his name only through a handsome bribe of the conductor. When I let on that I knew his name, he would simply stand and retire to his cabin, where even I dared not disturb him. I was like a farmer with a cattle prod, and I simply did not know when to stop—it was just too fun. It was almost sadistic how much I enjoyed prodding him and attempting to coerce secrets from him, of which there appeared plenty. And he is a curious man in more ways than this.

In one instance, I walked into the lounge car at the rear of the train and saw him drinking some exotic beverage. I could not exactly prescribe a color; it was some mix of orange, blue, and green. It contained alcohol, though he tried to hide it. I have been around my share of underground breweries and moonshine sheds throughout my career, and know the snappy scent very well. When he noticed I had taken notice of the beverage, he quickly tried to conceal it by foolishly putting the liquid in his jacket. The collision of his shirt-covered-body and liquid-filled-glass caused the drink to jump from the cup. It proceeded to leak down his side, until, in an almost comical fashion, his face turned red, and he threw the glass on the floor, where it exploded and sent streams of liquid and shards of glass in all directions. I was appalled when my shoes became the slightest bit moist. What's worse is that in his fury on his way out of the car, Marty practically knocked me over. I looked like a baboon in front of some of the country's wealthiest, who scoffed at me as I were the perpetrator.

After this incident, I began to think that my humorous treatment of Marty Turner was too sophisticated a type of comedy for him to realize, and that I should attempt to make amends with the sorry excuse for a man. After all, one cannot hunt criminals effectively if one is thought to be a criminal himself... Who in their right mind would hire me! It was not an easy task. But by this time, it was quite late on the 16th, and I had little appetite for being kind to a fool. I decided over a rare cooked lamb chop and apricot salad that evening that I would begin the next day with unparalleled morals and do my best to show Mr. Turner a kinder side of myself.

I stood up from my dinner and thanked the attendant—I think that is what they are called on trains—then walked a few cars down to my compartment. When I entered, I was met with my usual mess. Newspapers and magazines were strewn across the cabin, all originating from my suitcase, which had the dedicated purpose of carrying such documents. I opened my eyes wide and remembered that my payment was somewhere in the mess.

After a few minutes of searching with my hands and legs on the floor, I rested against the side wall with payment in hand—relieved. The train rumbled on through Big Sky Country. I thought I would have one last look at the stars, as it was something I hardly had the opportunity to witness because I so often found myself in the city. I put on more casual attire—though nice enough for the conductor to let me into the lounge car—and set out through the train.

It was a very different place at night. Its corridors

seemed endless, and the windows shook without speech to disguise the clatter. The train rounded a corner, and I fell against the window. My face was pushed up against the glass and I saw a herd of elk in the distance, staring at the glowing box which occasionally flew past them. How amazed they must have been. I continued walking through the hallway.

Clearly some compartment travelers forgot that they were not alone on the train and, in fact, were quite tightly sandwiched between two other cabins, evident by remarkable volumes of fornication.

When I got to the lounge car, I was amazed to find Marty Turner standing on the balcony at the end of the car. (It had a balcony! It must have been a very old car indeed.) He was not facing me, but he stared into the ether. The sky was like a mirror; it looked on Marty with the same gaze with which (I assume) Marty looked at the sky. The man was lost—I could tell—and I almost felt bad for him. The man had clearly experienced hardship, but I seldom had a clue of what it might be. Perhaps a nasty divorce, unbridled infidelity, or a shocking and sudden death in the family had rocked him. I could not put my finger on it, but it was surely devastating. I walked up to him, very quietly so that he was not alerted to my presence. I had studied some astronomy and was interested, for personal reasons, in the constellational patterns present in the sky. It was the summer months, which promised a new suite of star patterns. As the train thundered west, Turner and I gazed into the east.

Through the glass directly above my head, I saw

numerous formations. I always found the stars most interesting. Every arbitrary grouping was associated with some story from the classics. And somehow, the constellations' meanings transcend time and have come to touch us even in our modern age.

As I got closer to Marty Turner—I did so very steadily and quietly—I realized he was reciting a passage; it was the same passage over and over again. Each time he said, My grace is all you need. My power works best in weakness. So now I am glad to boast about my weaknesses, so that the power of Christ can work through me (2 Corinthians 12:9). Trust in the Lord with all your heart; do not depend on your own understanding. Seek his will in all you do, and he will show you which path to take (Proverbs 3:5-6). If my people, who are called by my name, will humble themselves and pray and seek my face and turn from their wicked ways, then I will hear from heaven, and I will forgive their sin and will heal their land (2 Chronicles 7:14). And then he was silent.

It took me by surprise and I froze in place, wondering if by some mystical means Marty Turner had detected my presence and curiosity. By this point, I was roughly ten yards away from him, and he resumed his recitation. I could hear his chanting with ever-growing clarity. At last I was nearly five yards away from him, and he stopped again. This time, he looked up into the heavens. When his eyes locked onto the stars, he spoke with utter moral clarity, almost to the tune of a preacher or philosopher: 'Do you, Mr. Lawrence, know the story of Orpheus and the Lyre?' I responded I had known once, but at this solemn juncture in my life, I had all but forgotten it. 'Perhaps I can offer you some… direction.' I was taken aback by the wisdom with which he spoke.

'After Orpheus's nymph bride Eurydice was stolen from him and taken with the utmost cruelty to the underworld, Orpheus had no choice but to make use of his lyre and craft to retrieve her. He ventured into a very dangerous and seldom explored part of the ether, below the heavens and under the mortal realm. With great reluctance, Hades allowed Eurydice forth into the mortal realm. There is more to the story, but it is not material to my metaphor.' I was amazed by his insight; so amazed that I ignored the fact Mr. Turner had neglected to tell the part of the story which issues a moral and a lesson. Now he turned around and faced me. He vigorously walked towards me and placed his left hand on my right shoulder, and then turned back to the sky. He gestured and stabbed his long, gaunt hand into the heavens. His thumb stabbed my shoulder.

'When you look at those stars and see the Lyra, think of Eurydice, and that she is perhaps no myth. Maybe, just maybe, she is a real person (his eyes were wide open, and I could see deeper into him than ever before) from a story in the present, and stars have aligned only recently to tell her tale.' Looking back, his blabber made no sense. He was clearly rocked from some relationship turned bad, though he spoke about it only in grand metaphors, which had only a momentary impressive effect. It passed, and with it, my interest in the conversation. I assured Marty that I would think on the issue for a night, and talk again with him in the morning. He seemed relatively satisfied with this answer and took his hand off my shoulder. He returned his line of sight to the floor of the rumbling train and quickly walked by me, brushing my arm in the process.

The whole incident occurred quite rapidly, and I found myself shocked because of it. I returned from the lounge car still half-dazed and began to record my thoughts. Perhaps in my attempts to make amends with the man the following day I will make reference to the constellations, biblical passages, and classical metaphors, as he did this evening to me. As I write this, I am shocked by the superstitious person one must be to ascribe merit to such things; how drunk he must have been. We were, after all, out of the middle ages. Marty Turner, I thought, ought to be out somewhere in a large city making a name for himself. He seemed like a half decent man.

*Noon on June 17th*—I have tried, but regrettably failed, in my attempts to associate and make amends with the man. I rose early, hoping to find a quiet moment in the dining car with him, but the fool stood me up! I sat there for many hours, drinking far too much orange juice than is likely good for my health, and many times had to persuade the steward to allow me to remain for just another few minutes; it was quite the embarrassing morning.

When the clock on the end of car hit 10:00 a.m., I was quite fed up and pronouncedly stood, tossed my napkin on the table (nearly knocking over my juice), and made my way back to my compartment. I was some complex combination of flustered and frustrated. I had, for the last few hours, made every attempt that I could to mend the wrongs which I inflicted on the man the previous day; none prevailed! It was absurd. I decided to take matters into my own hands.

With great resolve, I opened the door to my cabin and walked some cars towards the engine to another Pullman where I believed Mr. Turner to be sleeping and going about his business. I was appalled as I walked by the fornications which continued well into the day. How utterly uncivilized these travelers must be; it must just be their way in the West. I finally arrived at the car into which Marty Turner disappeared many times before. I opened the door and found a narrow hallway which ran the length of the car. In the middle was a door which apparently opened inward.

I reluctantly reached for the door knob; it was locked. Not only did the man refuse my attempts to apologize, but he also isolated himself in his car, sequestering himself from the world. But I was not deterred. By this point, I was rather set on seeing my apology through. What must one do, I asked myself, to be so wealthy that he or she could stay in such a large cabin?

No more than an hour later, the train stopped in Laramie. I found it a bit odd, and concluded the train must have made some unusual stop the previous night; normally the train between Cheyenne and Laramie is no more than a few hours. I took the opportunity to inspect his carriage from the exterior.

Much to my surprise, while the rest of the train had a stripe moving across it and was painted a dingy yellow-cream color, no stripe put a belt around Marty Turner's car, nor was his car the same color. In fact, it was an opaque green with gold trimming.

The only explanation, I thought, was that this was no train car. Mr. Turner must be so wealthy that he could fix his private carriage to the train. This was quite possible, so long as bribable officers were on duty at the time. Some of them were so stuck up with their morals; no fun for the rest of us. The curtains were also drawn at every window. There were slivers between some of them, but the sills were far too high for me to reach, and I refused to be caught climbing a train car to peek in the windows, making a fool of myself in the process.

For a few minutes, I walked about the platform. The conductor of the train, who was oddly young for a conductor, leaned against one car, elevated by the platform between two cars. He was an eagle eyeing his wayward prey. And he carried a smug grin on his face, as if he knew better than all of us combined.

All the wealthy women stayed on the train. They traveled only in their Sunday best, with hats and fans and the whole ordeal, so there was little point in messing it up by disembarking. Only the quasi-lowlifes, myself included, were inclined to step off for a moment. I walked up and down the platform, kicking rocks and such for ten minutes before the whistle blew and it was time to board once again.

Once the train was once again thundering towards San Francisco, I took refuge in my cabin, solemn as it was. But when it came time for lunch, 12:30 p.m. or so, I resumed my courtship of Marty Turner, this time with some mild success.

I found him sitting alone (not unusual) at his favorite table. The car rocked back and forth on the tracks, and the chandeliers swayed accordingly. Our meals jiggled on their china-plates, and the occasional thud! in the tracks caused drops of liquid to jump from cups and draw pointillism art on the white table clothes. It was all very grand as I took it in.

When I walked to him to sit down, he promptly looked the other way and motioned to leave. 'Wait, I beg you, please,' I asked him. He reluctantly looked at me, with a great deal of pity. 'Why should I? You have been nothing short of a wretch to me.'

'As I am aware, but I have come to make amends. Though I know in the early hours of yesterday I was cruel, that is not my better side.'

'Your better side should die.'

'Pardon?'

'What is a better side worth if evil and cruelty consume you in the end? Make it easy on yourself; beg for hell like all the fools around us beg for heaven. Live your life in the present as cruel as can be, with sure knowledge of your destination.' I was quite appalled by what he said. I was disgusted; he had inflamed my faith. I countered him with a long-winded explanation of the goals of the church (of which I was not a frequenter, but attended often enough that I knew a thing or two) and the logic behind its doctrines. He simply chuckled.

'Mr....' he said.

'Well, Lawrence,' I said in quite a dignified manner.

'Do you believe that we are all here for a reason?'

'Well, of course. It is paramount to my belief system.'

'So if I may be so intrusive: what brought you here?'

'Well, I'm on this train to find work in the West; after all...' He cut me off.

'Perhaps you misunderstand my question. I am not begging for an elaborate description of your work; I'm sure you do that quite well. Your persistence is remarkable,' he said this sarcastically. 'What unfortunate chain of events in your past led to be alone, on this train, talking to a lunatic, and hunting criminals? (So he had heard of my work!) Where is your family? Where are those you love? What brought you here, to this sad and desperate situation?'

# XIII

## LOG OF ARTHUR LAWRENCE

*Evening of June 17th*—And so it was last night that I told Marty Turner my story in its totality, from the very beginning to now. I thought the eventful part was in my early teens, before I made off to find my way in the world, but Turner was fascinated only by my later teen years, in which I was on the run, from sun up to sun down, without exception.

But afterwards, I think he had found new respect, and looked at me with almost an odd sort of yearning. Once I began telling my story, and he discovered it was about an escape away from everything that I knew, he was all the more fascinated. He looked at me eagerly and encouraged me to go into the most fine and minute details. I did find it odd in the beginning... Why is this man, clearly so well established, interested in a tale about a vagabond? It baffled me, but I came to appreciate the attention.

And so, after that fateful lunch, we became rather

close. We spent the remainder of the day together, playing cards and talking about our home lives—more Marty's resolution than mine. He was fascinated by my work, and I was obliged to inform him. There was no end to the questions about bandits and murderers and kidnappers and the like. He had some prefixed fascination, but who was I to deter him. I told him the stories of the Reign of Terror which had descended on the Osage People, and murders I had solved in that case, and of bank thieves in Wyoming.

Our conversation took us deep into our game of poker, which Marty was quite skilled at. He was much less blunt than I was, and seemed to approach every hand and flop with refined tactics and strategy. Just as we had broached and spoken about my line of work, I was equally interested in his. But when I brought the subject up for discussion, his face drained of color and his brows drew together. He took a breath in through his mouth, and his eyes remained fixed on his cards.

I was well aware that I had just made amends with the man, but his secrecy had sparked my curiosity, which is apparently a destructive force unlike any other. I would get to the bottom of this, I said at the time. Little did I know how deep he really was.

'Oh, well, I'm not really sure if I am at liberty to discuss my current assignment.'

'Sure you can! I just revealed to you much information, which could practically get me killed. Imagine if the authorities knew I was releasing such classified information to a...'

'A lawyer, I suppose I can at least tell you that I am a

lawyer.'

'I think that's alright. We are both men of the law. Just on different sides of the coin. No, wait, that is not an apt metaphor. More appropriately, we are like two different coins, and when both coins land heads-up, then the law is successful.'

'While I appreciate your flippant metaphor, for better or worse, I am not a criminal lawyer. I litigate for the finest companies and groups in the country at the firm of WINSTON & CO.'

'You know… you may believe to the end of the edge of the earth that practicing civil law precludes you from dabbling in the criminal world, but if I have learned anything in my years on the road, it is that evil has no boundaries. It's like a virus which spreads throughout the body, until it inevitably dies from corruption of morals. Sad, but true.' Marty Turner stared out the window at this comment. He bit his bottom lip and nodded slowly. A heavy sigh. He put his cards down and excused himself for a moment to use the lavatory. This gave me all the time I needed to extrapolate his reaction into a million different theories of the case. But despite my rampant speculation, I still held respect for Mr. Turner. There was a certain dignity I saw in him when he refused to immediately make my acquaintance.

I excused myself from the car and told the server that if Marty came back, and in a surely conditional statement, to tell him that I was called away on urgent work (while the reality was I was called away on pure curiosity), would be in my compartment doing work, and that he was welcome to disrupt me for any reason.

After a few minutes of jotting down my wildest theories, I turned to the few paper folders which I had collected in my bag. They were, in a most literal sense, my work. They were the villains and bandits who had bounties on their heads. And the more challenging it appeared to catch the bandits, the more money I would be paid for their heads. The key, though, is noting that the bounty is determined by apparent difficulty. Hardly a single government official I know has put their boots on the ground and taken bullets to the leg. Finding a criminal is as easy as finding one's own mother. All one must do is rely on their family, but there were few people who understood that, so the bounties remain quite high, not that I complain.

I picked through the various folders I had accumulated over the years. There were the property crimes, like theft and burglaries and heists. There were statutory crimes like drunkenness, but these types of crimes were so prevalent that even had I caught them all, I would still hardly made ends meet. And there were the personal crimes: assault, arson, rape, abuse, homicide, and the like; this, for lack of a better cliche, was my bread and butter. So I opened the manilla folder and began parsing through the individual papers. Needed something in the West, something high paying, something quick... Some I found interesting. And while they were a bit beyond my capabilities, the FBI's most wanted list was a gold mine for individuals in my line of work.

B. Parker & C. Barrow—Murder and Armed Robbery—$70K

G. Nelson—Murder and Armed Robbery—$65K

C. Floyd—Armed Robbery—$55K

A. Barker—Gang Affiliation and Leadership—$67K

Unknown—Murder and Bootlegging—$80K—murders and known associates in Great Lakes Area

The most wanted list was a dream, and in the moment, none of the more local criminals piqued my interest, so I set the folder aside and went about my discretionary reading for a period of time before there was a knock on my door.

I half hoped that it was Marty Turner, and was reluctantly happy when I opened the door and it was Marty Turner. I greeted him, but hardly could have invited him, given my tight space and the prevalence of my papers strewn about everything. He, of course, understood this as the gentlemen I more and more realized him to be.

'Would you like to head to dinner now? I heard that they are serving lamb tonight, and while I do love a chop, I am not sure that it is something which I would consciously choose to serve... Not everyone feels the same way about lamb, you know?' I did know, but I was one of those people. Ever since my childhood, when I consumed the Bible, I had a peculiar aversion to eating lamb. I know some might consider that a pagan practice, something more attune to Hindus and their aversion to cows, but I thought the matter was actually quite simple. So I bit my tongue and accepted his statement as truth.

He stood outside my compartment with his back to me for a few minutes while I assembled the necessary clothing for a meal.

'Looks like lavender,' Marty chuckled to himself. So we walked down the car's narrow hallway, I behind him. The carpet was so thick that I could hardly hear my footsteps, even though I wore my finest shoes which typically clicked and clacked like the finest tap-dancers of the era. When we got to the dining car, he held the dark, oak door for me, and I entered the room. There was a new decadence to it all now that I was there with someone else. The chandeliers shined a bit brighter and the silverware was all the more opulent.

We took our seats and ordered our meals. Like any half-decent dinner, it began with leagues of small talk… about the train, about the compartments, about the service. Looking back, I am surprised that the conversation, which began with such irrelevant talk, ended in something so gruesome.

The servers approached us with the menus and not long after, a feast descended before us. I admitted to Marty that I had something against the consumption of lamb. So he sat with his dish in front of him, embarrassed as can be, and refused to eat it. He ate the salad and potatoes that surrounded the chop. He even ate the sauce off of its top. But he refused to touch the lamb itself. It seemed that somehow, my comment had imbued in him a certain respect for the animal and its origin. I knew he was quite religious, or at least well-read in clerical literature, but I hardly expected him understand my superstitious motives for refusing to consume the lamb. But he did, and I was quite impressed. Seldom had a man sought to understand me before in the way Marty Turner did.

The train had stopped, once again, for some unknown

reason. It was like we were frozen in time, on a machine meant to float across the country with the same image out of our window for hours on end.

We discussed fine things: literature, current events... things of that sort. I'm not particularly of the mind that any of it was too interesting, but in the moment, the platonic connection between us forced me to care. We conversed late into the night. Eventually, we stood and made our way back to the sleeping compartments, just as clear in mind as we went into the dining car. But when we arrived at my door, and I reached into the nook to slide it open, Martin reluctantly pursed his lips and said: 'Would you be interested in something a bit... lawless? I know that you're likely averse to such indulgences, but given the current... circumstances, I think you'll find it... less objectionable.'

'As long as you don't plan to murder me and I'll be able to move tomorrow not petrified by some obscure poison, I don't see how it could hurt me.' Quite obviously, I do not come from the most wholesome or guided past, but from my shanty childhood, I crafted morals. And while I normally steadfastly stand by those morals, for whatever reason, I was overwhelmed by some obscure force. It confounded me, but even not knowing what my future held, I had no objection. And had I known what I know now, I am not sure if I would have changed too much.

I accepted Marty's offer and followed him down the hallway to the door which I had approached before. But instead approaching the door and finding it locked as I had done prior,

I approached behind Marty. He led the way, shielding me from what was to come; while now it may not have seemed necessary, at the time it surely was.

I entered the car. Several things struck me immediately. First there was a man standing in the corner, behind an ornate bar. He was dressed in white, from head to toe. Like a statue, or like a ghost, I could not decide. Behind him there was a wall of shelves: bottles upon bottles of all shapes and sizes and colors and heights. There were liquids of exotic shades of blue and green. There were couches made of a heavy maroon fabric. The cold marble floor had raw umber rug strewn over it; the tassels were scraggly and disorganized. It was the only part of the room I would have criticized. Most striking of all, however, was the scent. The poison, to which I was previously exposed, slithered up my nose and stuck pins in my brains. My nostrils flared open, despite my body's obvious disregard for the stench.

I stood inside the car and told Marty a story; perhaps it was a fictitious anecdote I conjured amid my amazement of the room... After all, I often read tales, and often they are easier to accept than the realities I often face: 'There was a certain fellow who came from the mountains. He was the mightiest in the land. I was afraid, so I did not go up to him. He filled the pits which I had dug as traps and wrenched out the traps that I had spread for his criminal friends. He released the other criminals from their wild jails, and he prevented me from doing my job in the wild.' The walls of Marty stood around him; the whole room assembled about him.

Marty walked over to the bar and pulled down a large

bottle. It was cylindrical in shape, and contained a caramel liquid. It was transparent like water, but possessed a slightly lesser viscosity. Marty twirled the bottle with a twist of his wrist, and in the yellow light of the lamp, it looked like liquid gold.

'I know it's likely a rather litigious form of pleasure, but please—I hope that you can set aside your scrupulous morals for an evening and imbibe. I can tell you my story eventually... maybe, and how I got here (he shrugged at this, suggesting there was some degree of complication, but I was aware of this from the outset).' Marty spoke assured, but simultaneously understood that his statements were indeed questions.

I was flustered. And overwhelmed, not by pressure, but by circumstance. I was overwhelmed by the gold ornaments and the long, satin curtains. I was overwhelmed by the tassels, erect like branches, and I was overwhelmed, most of all, by the presence of another whose illegal actions I was, for the first time in my life, willing to overlook in the name of conversation. 'Marty, you're surely well aware you could get yourself in quite a heap of trouble if you were to be—have been—found with such liquids...'

'Yes, you're right. But I assume that risk willingly, and really, without any other options. Perhaps I could tell you why, but only if you take a sip.' His grin was not obvious, but suggestive; it did not range from cheek to cheek, but from edge of lip to edge of lip. It was small, but impactful.

And so I drank! Yes, I admit it, and I do not know why. Looking on the events of only hours ago, my actions were irrational. It was like I was a puppet, and some unknown part of my own mind was the puppeteer. It was a strange sensation. I was a virgin to the stuff, so I did not know what to expect, or how to drink it, or what to ask for, or even what to drink! So Marty poured me a glass of whiskey, and the devil stung my tongue and lips as it rolled between my cheeks.

The mood suddenly changed, the candles glowed brighter, and I was more susceptible to evil than I had ever been before. I spoke loudly. 'This is the Devil's work!'

'How dare you say such things! It is merely out of necessity.'

'If it is out of necessity, why do the lay people no longer imbibe?'

'They don't know how!'

'What? What do you mean they don't know how! If anything, the lay people should imbibe the best.'

'No, you can't trust them with the stuff.' Marty said with a ridiculing tone.

'Why not? Don't they need it more than you in your cushy train car? They are the ones who need to face the trepidations of life and work and trade.'

'That is the easy conclusion... but they use too much of the stuff.' Now smugly, he offhandedly remarked: 'But why not, they're profitable as all hell, I'm told.' And things became a morsel clearer. I squinted at him and watched as Marty continued to drink without limitation. Glass after glass of what I thought to be among the stronger of the liquors the bartender offered flowed up into his mind. Perhaps it did the same to my own brain.

An hour in, I could not tell whether the train was wobbling on a bridge, or if I had simply had more to drink than the good Lord ever intended me to. Regardless, all seemed well, and I actually learned a few things about Marty. Our conversation went like this:

'So, you say that the lay people are... profitable?' I said.

'Yes, but perhaps in doing so, I overstepped my balance. You'd better disregard that comment.'

'Mr. Lawrence, you must be aware that, as a result of your last statement, I am more intrigued than ever in the matter, and, in fact, I am actually encouraged to probe even deeper.'

'I beg that you...'

'No, what is it that you do?'

Arthur let out a sigh of resignation: 'Many things.' He smiled, still trying to prop up his defense, but I was honing in on him, like a hunting dog on a fallen duck. I would arrive in a minute or so.

'If I recall correctly, you're a lawyer... Is that incorrect?'

'No, you are most correct in that assumption, seeing as, if I recall correctly, I told you so!'

'And because of the dubious nature of your indulgence...'

'I beg your pardon! What is dubious about the occasional drink?'

'The Devil.'

'No!'

'Why not? Don't you feel the Devil too? In your mouth? When the drink washed back and forth?'

'No!' His repetition of the phrase portrays my hostile nature quite accurately.

'God save your soul.'

'Thank you. Next time I speak with my boss...'

'Ah! So that's it! You are a lawyer employed by a boss of some sorts. What is he—a gangster, or a taxation evader, or...?'

'I think that your imagination is running amuck. You best reign it in.'

'A pimp, or a bootlegger, or...' but I stopped here, as something I had said clearly piqued his interest.

So I repeated: 'Pimp? Bootlegger?' As I said bootlegger, something gave way in him. It was not a blatant giveaway; perhaps something in the posture, or something in his eyes. But it was a tell, and I had struck gold.

'So to summarize,' I inquired, 'you are a lawyer employed by a bootlegger to do... what?'

Marty sat on the couch, defeated, drink in hand. 'You might as well have it all, as you already have plenty to shut me away for a while.' Marty stood and sauntered to the small table that had been temporarily rearranged to serve as a desk. Several times, shifting though stacks of paper, he almost knocked his drink over. Finally, he threw a bundle onto the ground which made a hefty thump and held up a single envelope to the light, as if to inspect it for purity. The man had gone crazy.

He returned to his seat. 'I will need this soon to complete my narrative of the recent weeks. It will validate to you the unbelievable tale which I am to tell you, with things so fantastic they should only be heard by the most emotionless of men—for you may very well swoon. It is a real possibility, one which I experienced first-hand.

So the story began.

# XIV

### FILES OF MARTIN TURNER
*(As found aboard the train upon entry)*

Dear Mr. Turner,

If I am correct, and I believe I am, it was Dostoevsky who wrote, "Pain and suffering are always inevitable for a large intelligence and a deep heart. The really great men must, I think, have great sadness on earth." And perhaps, ironically, you are a great man. And what I know you have seen has surely weighed on you significantly; when I first saw, I too was in awe. But I have come to accept the nature of the woman I love, for all the quirks she possesses. I thought you might appreciate an acknowledgement that you are not alone in that... but I digress.

It is not every day you uncover secrets of the magnitude which you did. At the same time, though, I am inclined to think that it might be even a bit fun... sleuthing, if you will.

But my abstract understanding of your current state is more or less irrelevant. After all, you were employed for a purpose, and I intend to use what I have paid for. By now, I am confident you can comprehend why we are such a profitable institution. The ability to artificially suppress our deepest and most haunting fears is practically a gift... Why the government keeps it to themselves, I do not know. All the better for us, I suppose.

But to business...

We had an unfortunate hiccup some time ago. A rather disobedient rail worker decided that he could rob us of our gold—figurative, of course. He took it from our trains and loaded it into wagons. He towed his wagons up into the mountains like a goddamned pioneer and sold it to the Indians and hill people. Things took a turn for the worse for the poor man when he made a family business out of it, and his mother became the accountant and his sister the saleswoman and his brothers and father the ones who moved the stuff. What began a small scheme, taking only a few barrels to make a couple of dollars, turned into a criminal enterprise—they would take whole boxes straight off the train and reconnect the cars like nothing ever happened.

This, of course, could not stand. We had them disposed of accordingly, though not with grace; it was unfortunate indeed. Their deaths spread throughout the town, as did the family's deeds. But much to my chagrin, he appeared to have spread the idea of theft of our prized goods through the small town. Paradiso—in the foothills of the Sierra Nevada—is a goddamned deplorable camp for the beggars. But as a result, the entire town is now profiting. They are building new houses and have gardens with lilacs and roses. There are farms that have sprung up, solely to house my property in their silos and barns. The children now have schools and the people can eat... all because of their thievery. Honest to God, man, it must end!

We could just as easily burn it to the ground and do what we did without initial thorn. But I would much prefer to deal with this problem constitutionally. Simply destroying the town as the great flood once did earth would not stop the problem. Surely others have heard how lucrative thievery can be; it would simply persist elsewhere. And by now, I trust that you have realized that we much prefer to keep our name less well-known—and leave it to mystery as to who gives the people what they truly want. As such, you must go to this town, and somehow and by some means persuade them to stop seizing my product and selling it off to people who live in the ungodly shanties around them. You may offer them money, within reason, but you would be remiss if you thought I had not already attempted to do so.

I care not what measures you take, so long as bloodshed does not stain me and my gold makes it to the Pacific Ocean. I know this is not likely what you envisioned when you came under our employment, but I do hope that you will find the whole thing rewarding—from a monetary perspective, I know you will. Personally, I am not so sure.

I know that you are a good man, a virtuous one too. But before my checks meet your pocket you may need to stretch your boundaries. It is the only way you'll succeed in your field and be truly exceptional. But, like my good man said, pain and suffering are inevitable—it's a truth!

Ekaterina and I will come to California to check your progress come the beginning of the next month. We have a small house only a few hours away; I do hope it is well maintained. We are somewhat of an urban legend in the area. Perhaps you too will get to go down in this awful and pitiful history of the Paradiso.

In this folder and throughout the car, you will also find enough money for fine lodging (if you can find it—I am not sure it exists) and food, as well as clothes and any other miscellaneous expenses you might incur. It will surely be enough. Any remainder you may keep as gratitude for your thrift.

I wish you the best of luck in this endeavor; it will not be easy... Believe me, I have tried. But a fresh and relatively independent perspective on the whole thing could, perhaps, crack open the problem like a fresh egg.

Godspeed, Turner.

Sincerely,
O. Aesterna


LOG OF ARTHUR LAWRENCE

*Morning of June 18th*—It is a true shame that I abandoned my morals and drank to my depressed heart's content. This day has been a tragic one, a haunting one. The Devil has found me, and there is little, it would seem, that I can do to escape him.

It would be easy for me to conclude that my actions of the previous evening were wrong, not only because it was illegal and my profession forbade it, but because my strong morals had been temporarily sequestered—and the gut-wrenching outcome of it all spinning around in my head.

The plot of Marty Turner's life was also fascinating. The interest was more to do with my regret than any moral error. In my analysis of the situation, Marty, too, had once been good, corrupted by his vanity and his hubris. His childhood was simple enough, a young boy in the woods, not totally unlike myself, omitting the abuse and religious fanaticism, and his early career seemed like it was going well, until he met the Aesternas—damn! The opportunity...

The true reason why I am upset that I drank is as follows, and it has taught me never to make the same mistake again:

When I awoke this morning, I came to the grave realization that I had passed over an opportunity, and a significant one at that. After Marty told me the story of his time with the Aesternas and their wicked deeds, I quickly consulted my notes and files, which confirmed with confidence that they were, in fact, among the most notorious criminals at large in the country at the time—and to think that I was sitting there with one of their most trusted employees. Oh, how I would have loved to have made the connection at the time;

only, I was too drunk and my ears were half open. It was quite unfortunate, because when I returned to Marty's car (which I began to think was merely on loan to him), I found it locked, and despite all the knocking in the world, no one came to the door. I peered through the blurred glass but heard no life. I leaned my ear against the green painted door, but heard no sound. I concluded that the car was empty. At the time, I half doubted myself, but as I came to understand the rest of the situation, I found my suspicion to be correct.

Perhaps, I thought, he had revealed too much to me and destroyed all of his paperwork. After all, the one thing the boss begged was that there be no connections to his livelihood. And so I ran about the train frantically asking if anyone had seen the man, or even his bartender, who had stood in the corner, seemingly mute and deaf (I suppose that would mean that he had done his job well).

The waiters in the dining room had not seen him, which meant that, though the hour was early, he had not been to eat. There were men smoking in the lounge car (how disgusting), reading the morning paper, but none had seen Marty. I questioned attendants and other travelers, but none had seen him disappear, until I spoke with the conductor.

His suit was blue—a remarkably dark blue, bordering on black. He stood like a soldier and had the mannerisms of a soldier too. His nose was pointy, and his lips were long and narrow. The deep brown color of his eyes reminded me of fine redwood, and his cheek bones could practically pierce metal; they were so astute and pronounced. He spoke only in short phrases, four words at most, until breaking into a most eloquent narrative of the events which had transpired in the early hours of the morning.

'It must have been five o'clock in the morning when the man in white came rushing out of the locked car, which even I am prohibited from entering. He was panting, like a child anticipating the emergence of devils from the closet. It was almost comical how a man so falsely wearing his suit acted so out of character. He proclaimed: Now! Now! You must help now! He will not make it much longer if you wait; please help! I, of course, responded that I had positively no idea about whom he spoke of. The ambiguity of his plea dominated it. He explained to me that a Mr. Turner had swooned shortly after, well… you of all people left the car. He was quite frazzled by the whole ordeal, and rightly so. I followed him into the lavish car and saw Turner laying on the ground as if he had been murdered, though, without any bruises or bullet wounds. The booze on the wall hardly shocked me, as many a rich person has brought liquor aboard. But the sheer quantity this particular man had ingested, according to this gentleman in white who never revealed his name to me, was remarkable. Shots and shots, and glasses and glasses, and bottle after bottle… it was… remarkable. After we placed him in a comfortable position and he came to, he was quite confused. He asked what happened, and we informed that we (the man in white, and I) believed that he was unsuccessfully poisoned. For your good sake, Mr. Lawrence, he refused and said this had happened before. With what little conscious time he had, however, Martin requested that the train be immediately stopped and that he be taken to a hospital. The price he offered was well above our means, so we gladly accepted.'

'So as of this moment, Turner is in a hospital in the town?'

'Yes, I believe so.'

'And... what town are we in?'

'The great Salt Lake City.'

'And how does one get to the aforementioned hospital?'

'I can arrange for a car, if you'd like. Though, I am not sure if Mr. Turner will want to receive visitors in his current state.'

'Arrange the car.'

'Yes,' he said smugly—rolling his eyes.

And so sometime later, I arrived at the hospital, but not before I passed through a most despicable city. To my knowledge, the Saints had built the city some time ago, but did a poor job of it. To begin with, it was the Mormons who built the town, with their own cultish ways. I had to keep my head down to prevent them from proselytizing me. It was I risk that a truly ran by being there.

But despite its non-Christian origin, the city itself was rather pleasant. The snow-covered buildings were tall and the streets were broad. There were wide sidewalks with herds of people, bustling about. Perhaps best of all, mountains jutted up from the ground behind the city. The site was quite grand.

The car passed a large church, where hoards of people congregated outside. Some were praying, others seemed to just wait—for what I do not know. When I saw them, I was quick to duck my head. But before I did so, I made momentary eye contact with one of the Mormons, who looked at me like a siren and smiled. How cruel! They all try to seduce me with their faith—but I will be stronger. Just before we rounded the next turn, the doors opened and the crowd flooded into the building. I heard the faintest noise, like a choir, emerge from the hall. I rolled down my window to listen. Though we had just passed to the front of the church, we were now driving along its side, where the tall windows were open, rotated forty-five degrees on their long axis.

The building towered into the sky, and through the ajar windows, I caught a glimpse of one the largest choirs I had ever seen. The men wore blue robes, and the women, on the right, wore red robes. In the middle stood the choir master, whose lengthy white gown and hat made him larger than life. He stood on a raised platform, with the long staircase leading up to it behind him. He faced the choir with his hands raised— he was the greatest puppeteer I had ever seen. The volume grew:

*In the beauty of the lilies Christ was born across the sea*
*With a glory in his bosom that transfigures you and me.*
*As He died to make men Holy, let us die to make men free!*
*As God is marching on!*

We rounded the corner and the music faded out of earshot. For a moment, I was approached a state of near excitement. But the moment fled, and my godly fear of the church returned.

After a few more minutes of solemn driving, we arrived at the city hospital. Upon entry, the whole thing appeared quite sanitary—and sterile. The walls were white. The floor was white. The ceiling was white. But the counter was a kind baby blue. And the kind woman behind it, though I do think she was a Saint, was quite accommodating. The medicine, because we were in the Mormon country, was likely quite pagan in nature.

The kind receptionist nurse showed me to Marty Turner's room, but much like his car on the train, I found it locked. In no time at all, I grew quite frustrated. It was, perhaps, the only hospital door in the entire country which was allowed to be locked. By this point, I was set on gaining as much information from the man as I could, with the ultimate goal of apprehending his employer. It would be a victory unlike any other in my field.

But I could do none of it unless Marty opened the door. My face grew red, and I thrust my white-knuckled fists upon the cloudy glass, yelling his name with every bit of air in my lungs. The pane shook and clouded the distorted image further.

And from within the room a voice spoke: 'Go away, goddamn it! You have been told too much already. Lock us up if you must for the crimes that you too committed, but do so judiciously and move out of my life for good soon after!' I guessed this to be the voice of the bartender... my guess was correct. He came to the door and propped it slightly open, for the sole purpose of making scathing eye contact. His head was tilted back slightly. 'I should not have yelled, as Mr. Turner has grown quite sick... deathly almost, and I blame you for this misdeed.'

'That is ludicrous! You saw me the entire time I was in the compartment. How could I have in any way killed him? That assertion is mad!'

'You may think so. But this morning when he awoke, two things were amiss with him. First, because you were present, he drank so liberally that I have never seen anyone as intoxicated by the stuff. And secondly, he revealed far too much to you last evening than he ever should have. When he stood out of bed, he swooned with only the thought... so shocked by his nonchalant sharing of information. You forced him into both of these. And there are many things—many things—which you do not understand, nor will you ever likely understand, about the inter-workings of the house of Aesterna. Imagine, Mr. Lawrence, that I stood on the top of a tall building and dropped a small pebble straight downwards, perhaps with a slight force. But imagine also, that you stand directly below the pebble. It goes faster and faster and faster, until all of the sudden, a little pebble is falling fast enough to kill you. And it was all because of the forces of nature.

'I think that you best leave, seeing as we have detached our car from the train and will be staying here for some time until Mr. Turner comes by better health. And I am of the belief that your absence will hasten that process.'

'Why,' I asked, 'are you so bent out of shape about the whole thing? What personal affection do you possess for Mr. Turner?

He raised his eyebrows in my direction, pursed his lips, and shut the door, which landed only inches from the tip of my nose. How rude a man...

So for an hour or so, I sat just outside Marty Turner's room, waiting, for nothing in particular. I did not expect a sudden change of heart in the bartender, who, in a very conspicuous nature, stood by Mr. Turner's side—always. Several times, the man opened the door a sliver, to inspect the scene and see if I had disappeared yet. He did this several times until eleven o'clock, when, reluctantly, he opened the door completely and beckoned me inside without a word.

Like the rest of the building, the scene was quite sterile. Like the lobby, the walls and ceilings were white, and there was a window which faced the city. But the weather had set in, and the window was white with some combination of fog and haze—but still it was bright... a bright white. There were sky blue curtains which framed the window, and a fluffy and light blanket draped over the sickly body of Marty Turner. It was evident that only recently had he awoken from his deep Devil-induced sleep. His face was without color and he was, as a whole, rather gaunt. The pale skin was like the floors, but more dull, and less lit. When he spoke, his voice was distant, dim, and quiet.

'Arthur, please come close.'

'Yes, what has happened to you? You were so jovial only a few hours ago.'

'My friend, you must know some things that might put you at ease. I am sick, and I have been for weeks. I told that story of how I became sickly, and I am of the belief that when God saw how the Devil touched my soul, he abandoned me completely. I let go of his hand and fell... quite far... down. There is the house whose people sit in darkness (which he had told me of); dust is their food and clay their meat. They are clothed like birds with wings for covering. They see no light; they sit in darkness. I entered the house of dust, and I saw the kings of the Earth, their crowns put away forever—rulers and princes, all those who once wore kingly crowns and ruled the world in days of old. Then I awoke like a man drained of blood who wanders alone in a waste of rushes, like one whom the bailiff has seized and his heart pounds with terror. I have done much wrong...'

'Why do you sound so hopeless? I have known you only for a short while, but undeniably we have grown quite close. You let me in on your secrets, and I on mine. Why do you speak like death is coming for you at such a young age? Think of your fiancée, think everyone who you have ever known... Why do you act now as if you have nothing to live for?'

'My friend, the great goddess cursed me, and I must die in shame. I shall not die like a man fallen in battle; I feared to fall, but happy is the man who falls in battle. I have done awful things and caved to the most despicable people on this earth. I do not deserve to live for the things which I have done. I have released the hand of morality and fallen into hell.'

Tears came to my eyes, and I knelt beside him.

'Do me a favor,' Marty said.

'Yes, anything.'

'Find some paper and transcribe a letter for me... for Virginia, my fiancée, in Philadelphia.'

So I scurried around and located the materials necessary. I pulled close a table and chair, and became situated so that he might begin to speak.

# XV

LETTER FROM MARTIN TURNER TO VIRGINIA KELLY

Virginia,

I write to you from my bed, bound to it by forces beyond my mortal control. These weeks have not been kind to me. And for not writing, I have in turn not been kind to you. Kindness is cyclical, and I made the choice to stop the cycle—I suppose that is what it means to be man, to pervert the kind things in life.

There are tales to be told, but none of that is relevant to what I need to say now, that I am sorry. I have been a burden like no other. I abandoned you in a time when we were, together, supposed to prosper and enjoy our lives. I succumbed to my own dastardly greed and cowardice, and failed to stand up for the values and morals I falsely paraded around like my own.

I thought I knew what it meant to be good, but evident

by my actions, I never did. I am at fault and have hurt you because of it, though the intent to do so was never there—I assure you.

This is my resting place, I know. There will be a few more days for the hands of the world to reach out from in between the atoms in the air, and grip my naked body and drag me into the next life. Where I am bound, I do not know.

Should you choose to join me in my final moments, I would love you eternally, as much as one can when in hell. If you choose to move on, and create yourself anew, or exist as you do with aspects of you anew, I shall love you just the same.

The Aesternas have done awful things to me and ask that I do even worse things in return. Since I ventured to Chicago, life has not been scenic. As the fuse on my candle burns away into the ether, the poor player I am becomes even poorer, not only materially, but also morally. I am an idiot full of sound and fury, whose thoughts and values signify nothing at all.

With love,
Martin


DIARY OF VIRGINIA KELLY


June 19th—Sometimes it is challenging to express how complex—or complicated?—one's thoughts can be. The distinction between the two is subtle, but it surely exists, evident in me. Am I complex? Or am I complicated? I am not sure I will ever know the answer.

When I got Martin's letter, I all but felt to my knees in prayer. He said it clearly: our lives were ahead of us. The fragility of life has never been so apparent to me—and how one poor choice can swipe the whole thing away, like a callous and calculated hand of cards at the betting table. Worldly powers greater than myself, though some more evil than I can imagine, seemingly always have the ace tucked away in their sleeves somewhere. And if they lack a real ace, they manufacture one from their dubious profits. Acquiring that ace... that is the true evil in it all. And it would seem that in our one-on-one game, the powers played their cards and stole from us all we had.

I got the letter in the middle of the afternoon when I arrived home from my usual round of errands: first the book club (we were now onto something long... and Russian), then the church, and then the park. Quite routine. But when the clacking of my boots ceased at the door of our antique town house, and the wooden planks bent beneath my soul, I saw the envelope and knew immediately who it was from. Though it was of remarkable quality, I was more than sure the wealth which he was exposed to would give him access to such stationary. I could not help but to open it on the spot, in the bare air, humid as it was. The air surrounded me like an ocean, as it always did, but my tears made the calm sea stormy; I almost fainted standing there, and I could hardly imagine the awful things that he had seen. My initial reaction had proved correct—the perverted nature of his task had revealed its ugly face. It was Medusa and had turned Martin to stone.

I entered the narrow rectangle and sought refuge on the white, plush couch. I stared at the ceiling. The lights began to dance in circles, and the roses on the wallpaper died away, shriveling up into brown pods and falling off their branches. The leaves became tattered, consumed by a horde of ants.

And into the air I yelled: 'Why! Why! Why!' Tears streamed down my face and made dark splotches on the couch, graying the cloud upon which I sat. I turned onto my side, so my gaze was parallel to the floor beneath me. It was a dark wood, which had stood the test of time. Many storms have passed overhead since its conception, but it seems to have fared quite well. I laid on the couch for several minutes, dazed and confused by what had occurred. It was like a trance—but conscious simultaneously.

The fourth movement of Beethoven's Eroica Symphony rang in my head from a performance the previous evening I had gone to see with the women in my literature circle.

After some time, I awoke. Of course I would go to be by his side. I struggle to reconcile why he did not insist on my presence. But that has always been one of the great things about him: he is kind, never overbearing, and he knows his place in my life.

Within minutes, I had emptied my drawers of the clippings I had collected over the weeks of his absence. Perhaps, I thought, these could be of some use to Martin, since his awful time in Chicago corresponded remarkably with the deaths of so many youths in the same area. I cobbled together a suitcase of clothing and mementos—and cash.

In the closet, I found my favorite traveling dress. It was thick, but breathable. It provided protection from the forces of nature but never suffocated me. Suitcase in hand, I marched through the miniature foyer and onto the porch. There sat two white chairs with a small white table in between. They were worn by nature but not use. As I stood, I had a vision of what could have been. If only...

In the little time I had left, I decided that it would be of the utmost importance that whoever composed the stories about the missing individuals in that area be informed that it was perhaps due to the misdeeds of the Aesternas, whoever they might be.

The cab drove quickly enough, but when I arrived at the office of the Philadelphia Inquirer at 6:00 pm, the service could not have been slower. There were few lights on, but I knew that some diligent reporter would accept my task; they were all just looking for their break in life. There was a woman at the front desk, but she was preoccupied with something bureaucratic and said several times to me 'hang on, honey, for a second.' Unfortunately my business could not 'hang on, honey, for a second,' so with my head held high and suitcases in hand, I promptly marched by her. Needless, to say, there was surprisingly little objection.

The hallway was short, thankfully (given how I was weighed down by my luggage). I passed several individuals in offices who stared, but I did not care. How comical the image must have been: a woman in a large dress and overcoat carrying luggage through a newsroom. Eventually the short hallway, which turned out to be more an entryway, opened into the real newsroom. The walls were yellow, and the large concrete pylons reminded me of a prison—not that I had ever entered one. Here, I thought, I will find someone who will appreciate what I have.

But while there were not too many people crouched over their desks punching out lines on their typewriters, no one seemed to have noticed my entrance. So I dropped my suitcases on ground, with a great thud! This caught their attention. So, like their editor, I announced to them all: 'I have information regarding a series of murders in the city of Chicago... or in the area or Chicago... or that part of the country. Out of the corner of my eye a young man picked up the phone, but other than that, not even one finger lifted. So I stood there, and time froze as the heads returned to their lowered positions.

I seized my suitcases from the floor and swiftly swung them around. I took a step away from my previous position. But as I did so, I heard a fluttering of papers in the background and clicking of shoes on the tile floor. Given that I was in a newsroom, I thought little of the noises—until a female voice violently whispered 'pardon me, pardon me, pardon me.' I swung around once again to see a colored woman in her early forties weaving through the labyrinth of desks and typing machines.

She spoke to me: 'I'm sorry for the brevity, but I just got a note that said you had something about crimes in the Northwest?'

'Yes, I do… Are you familiar?'

'I have been there many times to report on the crimes which, I assume, connect to the material you have.'

'May I ask your name?'

'Hannah Herrman. I'm the Great Lakes reporter at the Inquirer.'

'Oh my! I've read your columns in the newspaper many times! Unfortunately I am on my way to the station now, to join my husband who was hurt the people which the letter makes mention of. I would give you the letter to keep but…'

'Can I come with you?' she asked abruptly. I was shocked by the question, and while I had no objection to traveling with a woman of color. what might people think?

'Well… I'm…'

'I realize that there are certain… reasons that you might be disinclined, but I can pay my own way, and would make good use of the opportunity. If the information you have, Ms.…'

'Kelly;'

'Ms. Kelly… is true, and it turns a lead, then, well… how the public would benefit from knowing. It would be truly remarkable.'

'I really don't think that would work too well. With all the luggage and… other things it may just not be feasible. I am not even going to the Great Lakes Area—your area!' I could not quite discern the expression which hung from her face. It was a combination of discontent and longing, I think. Her head was tilted slightly, and I know she spoke genuinely. I also failed to successfully discern why I initially declined her company. I was in no way... biased like many persons in the country (or at least I think I am not), and she seemed like a perfectly nice woman, competent, driven, and all. I suppose my denial rests solely in the reasons for my travel—it was personal, not the kind of reason one shares with another.

'Ms. Kelly, I realize that you surely have some trepidations, seeing especially as I have only known you for a matter of minutes, but I assure you that I will be no burden. And as for your destination, I long for nothing more at this moment than to meet the man you speak of, who has presumably experienced these atrocities. A good journalist must always start somewhere. Please understand that all I do is shine a light on that which is dark. And as of now, there is a mystery many layers thick: I am the spotlight, and your fiancé is the beacon that will point me in the right direction. Please—I beg you.'

It should be known that at this time, I was in quite a hurry. The 7:00 train was on my mind, and if I could board it, I could likely make it to Great Salt Lake by the following evening. Ms. Herrman, however, would need to return to her home, which I assumed was quite far from where we stood. I pondered her words for a moment, but without any good and thorough reasons to turn her away, I reluctantly accepted her offer of companionship. She made a convincing argument, but I am not sure that that is the reason for which I was so agreeable.

'Ah! Thank you! I'll be just a few seconds.'

'Where will you ever find your luggage in a few seconds?'

'As I said, Ms. Kelly…'

'Please, call me Virginia.'

'Only if you call me Hannah!' She grinned. Her smile was very pretty; it is one of the most characteristic things I recall about her. 'As I said, Virginia, despite what others may subjectively think of me, I am objectively a good journalist, and a good journalist is always prepared to run on whim.' She retreated to the room from which she came, having abandoned all her papers on a side table. I had twiddled my thumbs for no more than thirty seconds when Hannah once again emerged from the same port, covered in a lilac coat, buttoned up the wazoo.

I was beginning to take a liking to this kind woman Hannah, not that I had ever disliked her. But she integrated herself into my life with remarkable speed. In the coach on the way to the train station, we spoke of politics and city planning. She had some particular convictions (which I understood fully, I think) that the government had done a great disservice to the colored population.

'Oh yes,' she said. Somehow, though I'm not sure quite how, she had come to the truthful conclusion that I was friendly to her kind—unlike most people of my day and from my part of town. 'I grew up in a small city outside of Baltimore and have battled Goliath ever since. It is partially what motivated me to become a journalist. I had a great deal of fun in my youth putting out publications with small articles on trivial things. Every so often something truly important would come up, and my friends and I would get a fire in our stomachs that not even the oceans could put out. It was truly remarkable. I've come to accept, sad as it is, that I will not in my lifetime be able to gain the recognition of some of the greats... If not because I am black, then because I am a woman. But who is to say that should stop my from trying? I will try and try until the fire in my stomach dies, but right now, in times like these—they keep the fire burning. And it is that fire that I rely on to shine my light on the world. It may not be the brightest or the greatest, but it is, objectively, the crispest image of a flame you will ever see in your entire lifetime.'

She spoke eloquently, and I enjoyed listening to her speak. She had a pastor's voice—at least the part related to meaning. She glowed with conviction. Even in my susceptible state, she kindled a small flame and passion for the truth. Just listening to Hannah speak, I was moved greatly—like a boat on a great wave of icy blue waters.

The car's wheels and my mind spun for several more minutes. We pulled up to the station and, with the help of our driver, unloaded our suitcases from the cab. Coats straightened, I checked my time piece: 6:34—surely we still had time.

'Well, I suppose I will see you at Great Salt Lake.' Hannah spoke with full sincerity.

'Why will I not see you on the train—or in five minutes?'

'Virginia, you are kind—very kind—but not everyone in this life is, especially not everyone in this city, or at this train station for that matter.' She smiled her beautiful smile and tipped her head back slightly, gesturing towards the entrance at the far end of the drop-off, where people of color streamed into the building.

'Surely I hope that I'll be able to talk to you again on the train. There must be some time or place where we can convene. I was just starting to enjoy your presence!'

She laughed, broadening her smile even more. 'I would love nothing more than to continue our conversations—especially given that even momentary separation from one whom you've just been introduced to is unbearable.'

Ah! And she was well read too. Now more than ever, I wanted to pick her mind and discover the nooks of knowledge contained within.

'Hannah, I will be sure to send word, perhaps we can meet under the cloak of night. I'm quite fond of platonic evening rendezvous. You best go now if you must, be sure to board the 7:00 train for Chicago, and from there we will transfer to the line bound for Great Salt Lake.' I gripped and squeezed her hands, and we both let out a small laugh and a smile.

Her coat blew in the wind behind her as she walked away. An image of grace, I thought, pure grace! The remainder of the evening was rather uneventful, until a particularly eventful conversation with the kind waitress.

As I got myself settled on the train, the attendants came through our compartments to inform us that a late dinner was being offered. Famished from a day of emotion and discourse, I saw it only proper to consume a hearty meal and prepare for the coming storm.

'Is the lamb any good?' I asked the woman, who wore

175

a long, green dress with her hair pulled back quite tight behind her head.

'If you are one for lamb, then the lamb is exquisite! But if you're not one for lamb, then I am afraid that it is not for you…'

'Well—how should I be expected to know if I am one for lamb or not? Your answer is quite circular and does not aid me in the slightest in choosing whether I should order the lamb, or the… what else is being offered?'

'This evening we not only have lamb, but other things too, if you can imagine it. And like I said, if you are one for lamb, then you'll find it extremely well prepared—though not well done, but also it can be well done. So would you like the lamb?'

'Ma'am, how should I be expected to make a ruling on whether or not to order the lamb if you have still neglected to inform of how it is cooked, let alone its marinade, or the side which comes with it?' I spoke candidly and honestly.

'I am afraid the lamb is not for everyone. Some individuals have a clear predisposition to it, and know that immediately they would like the lamb, but others… others truly struggle with it, and they do not know which way is up with the lamb. But I assure you, madame, that if you are one for the lamb, then you need not ask how it is cooked or what the sides which come with it are. If you are one for the lamb, my word enough should satisfy your need for the information—my word that if you are one for the lamb…'

'Then I will like the lamb! Yes, so I've heard!' I was

quite upset.

'With all due respect ma'am, I am beginning to think that you are not one for the lamb. If you cannot accept my word about the lamb, than there is really no way, I believe, that you can fully appreciate it. Those who are for the lamb order it, more or less, blindly. They take a great leap of faith. Perhaps their chop will be undercooked or over seasoned; they really have no way of telling.' She shrugged at this remark as to suggest some element of chance. 'You should know though, that everyone to whom I have ever blindly served the lamb has always enjoyed it. No question.'

I was quite frustrated that the woman dare to demean me... as if I were not one for the lamb. 'Very well, bring me the lamb! I shall taste it blindly.'

'Oh... well... I am afraid that those who are not for the lamb and who have ordered the lamb have taken quite little away from it. As such, I would really recommend something else, perhaps a more orthodox meal which you might find suitable. The most important aspect of the lamb is that you can never really know what will spontaneously emerge from the kitchen! It is a mystery! And solving the mystery is quite rewarding. But you, I am afraid, have already had the mystery spoiled for you, not by me, but by your own self. You see, in hesitating to order the lamb, you already took too much time to question it. It is no mystery because you have closed off your mind to more possibilities. You have one image of what the lamb must be. Though, I guarantee you the lamb is entirely another image... no doubt in my mind... no doubt.'

'Very well.'

'Bring me a steak.'

'Are you one for the st…'

'I am one for the goddamned steak! Now bring it here!'

Our conversation and relationship ended there, quite promptly. So be it, I thought, vile lamb!

# XVI

## DIARY OF VIRGINIA KELLY

*June 20th*—Hannah was right; the next time I saw her was in Chicago. I vastly overestimated the time which it would take for us to travel from Philadelphia to the Lakes. It was not long after 8:00 when the bell rang, informing us of an arrival impending. I finished gathering my items as the train pulled into the platform. The station was hustling and bustling with people, of all shapes and colors and sizes; it was a peculiar and strangely uplifting sight, as if the world converged in one building, knowing that in a matter of days or hours, each of the individuals I so admired would be on their way to or at their destination, some near, some on the other side of the world... with the invention of flight for transport, it was becoming more and more feasible. It was all very exciting.

I walked towards the front of the train to find Hannah. Because the observation car on this particular engine was at the back of the line, and it contained a smaller deck off the back, the colored section of the train was placed nearer to the front, so the white-folk need to pass through the colored cars on the way to their evening smoke or bridge games.

'How have you been? How were your accommodations? Did they treat you alright? I know you surely had some trepidations when you boarded the metallic behemoth to begin with!' I spoke quickly, worried for her.

'You worry for no reason. In fact, your worrying offends me slightly. Are you saying that I might not be able to look after myself? I am, after all, objectively, a very good journalist, and one does not get as far as I in the business, even as were a white man in his forties, without being able to take good care of oneself.' She half laughed, but did so with a profound seriousness. She meant what she said despite any facade she presented—this much I knew, so I was sure to not speak any more of it. Hannah, however, apparently had other intentions.

'Do you know how sandwiched together our seats are? It is profoundly unbearable. Like sardines really. It is the things like these which dig deep and leave marks. There was also no cool air or fans to move the air to and fro, so we sat there sweating like sardines in hot, muggy, and stagnant air. I'm relatively sure that our sweat evaporated, formed clouds above us, and return to our skin in the form of little beads of rain. I suppose the service was decent, though the water was of a questionable temperature. Virginia, I tell you, when things are left for me to do, by people whom I trust, which is most people—I am quite generous with my trust—I do them well. I do these things with diligence and propriety, even if they are for someone else. As long as I hold respect for a person, I will do as they please… because I respect them. But when people try to do things for me and do so half-heartedly… it is discouraging… so discouraging, and I do not take kindly to it. It is one of the few things in this life which I do not take too kindly to. I am sure that you'll come to see it and resent me for it too.'

'Oh I'm sure that no such thing will happen. I trust your convictions and know that they run deep and are grounded in fact and reason. We, literate women, have some responsibility to one another after all, right?' I took up a comedic tone, as I could not fully tell what her tone was. If I was serious, then I might kill the mood and our friendship, so I chose to be comedic, and in doing so, realized that my choice may have been the wrong one.

We ate a meal and talked more—some of literature. She was quite well-read, as was I. It was a mutual bond that brought us together quite closely. We walked towards our next train, quite inconveniently several platforms over (and we made the mistake several times of taking the wrong flight of stairs down the thing) when we passed a newsstand, bearing the headline: 'CHICAGO MURDERS CONTINUE.' It appeared that by the time this particular piece came to the forefront of the media, according the story, which I have handily clipped below, the authorities established several things: the killings take place in Chicago; the bodies are dumped into the Great Lake, the currents of which carry them to small town shores; the actual number of victims found in this particular way ranges from twenty to twenty-five; all the victims were murdered in quite horrific ways; some of them bled to death, some suffocated, some of them were drowned, and some smitten. It is all utter horror, no doubt.

But while this particular headline contained a great deal of summary, it remained centered on a particular murder, which seemed particularly horrible in nature.

CHICAGO TRIBUNE

'MORE BODIES FOUND WASHED UP ON GREAT LAKE SHORES'

The Federal Bureau of Investigation has discovered several more bodies, since taking over the case from local authorities early last week. They decided the crimes were of national standing. The individuals who perpetrated these crimes have been elevated on the FBI's top-ten most wanted list. The search for them continues.

The body discovered yesterday evening was a tall, fat man, with a neckerchief embroidered with the initials 'E.S.' If you are aware of anyone with these initials who is a missing person, please make a report to your local police department as soon as possible.

'This death is particularly chilling,' an FBI official said. 'While there was more done than meets the eye, we say for certain that the tongue was removed, and that the cause of death is the snapping of the neck. While the death itself was likely only painful for a brief moment, we are confident, based on other marks about the body, that there was significant torture involved prior to death. It is truly tragic and horrifying.'

# XVII

## DIARY OF VIRGINIA KELLY

*June 21st (on the afternoon of the 21st)*—Little to speak of for the remainder of the train ride. The Midwest is always a bore in terms of scenery. There's simply rocks upon rocks. The rocks, I admit, are of many colors and varieties, but seldom are they interesting enough to pique the interest of a passerby. They are all earthly colors, which are deeply saddening. Occasionally there is some grass, but little else.

Arriving at the hospital was like stepping into a dream. Never could I have imagined that the man whom I loved so dearly would act so negligently. He threw himself into his future, and there was little turning back. Futures do that—they grab one by the collar, take them in, and throw them out the back. Some say their futures hold opportunity, when, in fact, they had liability.

Momentarily, I doted on Martin, caressing his arm and sticking his poor and illness stricken face between my two cold palms. He was hardly conscious, so I was cautious not to push his mind. He needed rest; I was confident about that. My companion, however, Ms. Herrman, was apparently not under the same impression—much to my disappointment. In fact, she jumped on him like a lion does a rodent. It was utterly disheartening. I momentarily objected, but both parties, much to my chagrin, insisted that they speak. Neither knew each other, but their brief escapades in life bonded them. There was immediately some understanding, which I could not tell if I adored or despised—it simply was.

'Mr. Turner, it is my honor to meet you. I cannot fathom the things which you have experienced. For several weeks now, I've reported on the crimes in the area. On my way here—on the train—I read the letter which you sent to Virginia, and how I respect you for doing so. I'm not sure of how much help I can offer. I am simply a reporter of the facts, but the facts, for the most part, have been hard to come by, since no one ever lives, as the cliche goes, to tell the tale. I was hoping that you might shine light on the depravity which you have experienced, so that we all might learn a bit about the human form.'

'Ms. Herrman, I respect you immensely for your efforts and will tell you all that I know, but I ask only one thing of you... Anything which I tell you cannot be put out for the world to hear.'

'May I inquire as to why? Surely you're not still loyal to the people who have been killed by the town? Surely you must have had some change of heart in your journey? Surely you must have some sense of justice?' Hannah was quite flustered and understandably so. I admit that I too thought that there would be some change of heart which spun the moral needle in the right direction. Between the letters which Martin had written and the clippings which I had read, though I was sure I did not understand it all, I surely understood some, enough to realize that he had become a part of a world which I'd prefer he not even know. But Hannah's words upset me greatly; there was a kind of fire kindled within my heart, mind, body, and soul, which was not zeal for the truth, but desire to have the hellish tangle in our past. And all she did was prod so that it might continue to exist in the future—perhaps even live forever.

'You must realize that any action always has a reaction. I believe there is a law of physics which states this, or some other nonsensical jargon. And the action of treason against my employer... it would ruin everything. Everything! My career would fall to shambles... my pay would go to hell... and my name would be tarnished for eternity. I am fully aware of the diabolic nature of the Aesternas... Hell! I lived in hell with them for quite some time! They made it hell! But they are the puppeteers of commerce. In school, we learn about how scarcity drives supply and demand. But illicit things are, despite their being illicit, far from scarce. They are the devils on earth because they prey on the needs of the poor and profit from violence within the home. The Aesternas promote fights not just within their castle, but within households across the nation. Every time a man drinks the cool and pungent liquid, there is violence; there is unrest; there is pain. If I try to challenge the poor player on that stage, then there is no hope. I cannot bring down the puppeteer from above. I merely dangle from his strings. Perhaps I could somehow break the strings that control me, but then I would surely fall to my death in the holocaust below.'

Hannah was frustrated. I was more so. She stood there silently. The tension was palpable between all of us.

I coughed in the manner one does to discreetly attract another's attention; though, I was not too discrete. 'Ms. Herrman, a word outside?' I asked.

I held the door open and my head quite high as she exited the room with arms folded.

'Ms. Herrman, with all due respect, how dare you accost my fiancé in that manner? I know well of your profession, and I know well that the scoundrels in your profession often do such things. But I expect better from you of all people. He is a man wounded physically and in the mind, and for you to interrogate him like that—shaking your questions on him like pepper—it is disgusting, and I will not have it. Sure you can be... probative, but at what cost? At the present, we must help Marty put this episode behind him. We must block it from memory and move on with our lives. Can you see not that he is up against a giant, ten—no, one thousand—times his size? He cannot win; he is but a single man with only us at his side. They, by the looks of it, have an army bearing the finest shields and riches beyond our dreams. We cannot beat the beast, so we must do what we can to survive within it, and someday emerge victorious on the other side.' I spoke vigorously and steadfastly stood by what I had to say. 'Perhaps you should show yourself out. Clearly you have overstayed your welcome—or whatever the appropriate mannerism is for the situation.'

Hannah spoke: 'Ma'am, I cannot know where you stand, or how truly troubled you are by my actions but am disappointed in your shortsightedness.' She spoke bluntly, to the point where I almost backed down completely. 'You postulate that someday this giant will pass, and you will move on. I am of the mind that giants, regardless of their size, never truly leave us. We can beat them, kill them, and cut their heads off, but giants leave marks on us like nothing else in the world can. To think that by fulfilling his or that your husband will escape is foolish. A job well done will only encourage his employment again. A job poorly done... I ask that you draw your own conclusions. But to insinuate that somehow I am the one who is forcing this issue into the future is simply a fallacy. By doing what you think will put this stain in the past, you are simply perpetuating it into the future. I have learned in my few years on this hellish rock that the only way to move past giants is to bring them to their knees and cut their heads off (her voice was now quite agitated). Ms. Kelly, you may be surprised to hear this, but I too have faced my share of giants, and when they are not killed—a silver spike driven through their heart—they creep up, again and again and again, without remorse. You might think that you are the only one facing this particular heathen, but I assure you there are legions standing on the ground and staring upwards at the same figure. The giant is tall, Virginia, and it can be seen from everywhere in the world. But we, the people toiling on the ground, can hardly see past our own problems. I would encourage you to think hard—very hard—about your next steps in this... metaphysical proposition. I will do what I must to discern what I seek. At least one other person, preferably of the living variety, should know of the atrocities afflicted in hell. It is unfortunate for your fiancé that it is not you.' This infuriated me. The thought my husband-to-be would not admit to me his most hidden secrets rocked me. And the fact that the words came from the dark lips of Hannah Hermann exacerbated the situation. She continued: 'I will see myself out for the time being, but I am determined, Ms. Kelly, perhaps more than you. I am especially determined because, quite apparently, your myopia will render you unable to solve this problem.

'How dare you insult me in this way! I know you mean well, but you present like a... a... ahh! Be gone!' I spoke with ample frustration in my voice.

'I will be gone for a few hours, and I challenge you to think more succinct thoughts, to stare into the future, and realize the mess in which you've gotten yourself tangled.' In an instant, she had entered the hospital bedroom and emerged with her materials and with a cynical look. 'I'll be back. You'll come to realize you want me back.' And then, in an odd twist of events, Hannah smiled her gentle smile full of her pearly white teeth. It was the same smile that seduced me when I first met her. But there was a hint of pity in this particular expression. And for a moment, I considered taking her advice. But her lips shut with the same anger with which she spoke, and my consideration blew away in the wind with it. I remember little, only that as she neared the end of the hallway and the doctors and nurses pushing their carts began to eclipse her, Art popped out of a perpendicular passage, and as the two passed each other, there was a split second of acknowledgement. Hannah turned to face him, and looked him up and down. She clutched her purse, and keeping her eyes on him, hurried out of view. Art simply stood there, with all the muscles in his face completely relaxed. But just as quickly as the interaction had begun, it ended. Hannah was out of sight, and Art was moving towards me with a heavy bag of food in his left hand.

'Do you know her from somewhere? She was particularly unbearable a moment ago,' I said.

'Well... have you ever had a moment where... you think you might, perhaps, know someone? When you have not seen them in many, many years? Almost like... there was no chance you would ever see them again? But then they appear. It may very well be like that. But I am not sure. She does look quite familiar, I must admit.'

'Art,' we still stood in the hallway, 'will you give me a moment with Martin—in private?'

'Sure, sure, I'll just be out here.' I nodded to signal my gratitude. I entered the hospital room where a nurse was administering some kind of medicine. I smiled, and with a small nod dismissed her. She shut the door behind her.

'Marty... (no response)... Marty... (still nothing)... Marty!' It was a whisper-yell. All things of true gravitas cannot be yelled, nor can they be whispered.

Marty opened his eyes and began to chuckle, as if he

had deceived me and played a joke. Needless to say, I was not pleased in the slightest.

'Marty, I am sorry for bringing that awful journalist. She has done neither of us any good.'

'You ought to speak more quietly.'

'What do you mean?'

'When you speak and do not want someone to hear you speak, you should speak more quietly.'

'Do you mean to say that you heard our conversation?'

'Quite clearly.'

'Oh! I am sorry. I did not mean for you to hear any of the atrocious things she said. She has no clue of what she talks about. She speaks in metaphors and slanders and prose—that bitch!' I was infuriated.

'Well...' Martin spoke timidly. In my rage, I spoke over him, bulldozing his words like a rolling pin does dough. Perhaps my mind chose not to hear his slight objection, given that I had one perception of how the dough should be shaped, and he had another entirely.

'I think her analysis is correct.' This comment stopped the rolling pin in place.

'How do you mean? Are you insinuating that somehow, this fiend has spoken some semblance of the truth?'

'Virginia, herds and flocks know when they have to head home from the grass, but an unwise man never knows the measure of his own belly.'

'Dammit, Marty! Stop speaking in metaphors. I have had far too many metaphors already today... I cannot stand the metaphors!'

'My dear, I mean only to say that I have tried my hand in profiting from the illicit, and my stomach is full. It is time for me to head home. The struggle is, that there is no home. I cannot return to my old job by simply quitting my current contract—hell, they are the ones that proposed me for this mess in the first place! The only way out is through the gauntlet. I, or we, or some combination, would be ludicrous to think that my living this way is sustainable; it is not in any way. We can only do our best now to return to the stable from our pastures...'

'Metaphors, Marty, metaphors!'

'Yes... sorry. But in doing so, it will require that we push against, as reluctant as I am to say it. I am sorry that I have gotten us into this situation, but there is no easy way out.'

There was a long pause. Our eyes met, and he smiled, the same smile which I fell in love with. His lips quivered and single tears slid down his face, dotting the sheet below. 'I am afraid that I have done you a great disservice.' He turned to look out the window and gestured for me to open it. Framed against the bluest sky I have ever seen was a human form with wings. An angel, I thought. The wispy clouds saw the form pass in a matter of seconds.

'Virginia, do you see the clouds? A person can see many things in a cloud. But when push comes to shove, clouds are little more than water. Life can be reduced to a series of decisions, marred by deception and lies. I am afraid that with no intent, you have been deceived... by me, and I am sorry. I am so sorry that I have put you through all of this. I am afraid that there is little I can do in this life to make up for my sins, chief among them being dragging you into life's depths. I ask that you leave me.'

'Oh Martin.' Tears accumulated in my eyes. 'You know that I can do no such thing. It is simply not possible. Fate won't prove so mighty that God shall pronounce a death sentence on you, for both of us shall shortly go off from here...'

Martin chuckled: '...to hell.'

For several hours after that, we sat, staring at one another, gazing into each other's souls. There were times when we took the other's hand, and times when we could hardly bear to look at one another. And it was not long before the sky turned dark with the day's storm. Rain poured from the sky, and the streets below were drenched in God's tears. Rivers flowed through the city. Swept up in them were the scraps and trash of the urbanites. The streets are cleansed, I thought, but all the debris must go somewhere. My consciousness was summoned to heavy sorrow. If the sea took him, or a sword cut him, I would make someone pay. I took fate to be my equal— no question in my mind.

Eventually the winds blew so strongly that the dim bulbs in the hospital blew out, and Martin and I were left holding hands, in the dark, staring down everything and simultaneously nothing. It was the climax of our introspective hours. The black void showed me not what was real, a dark canvas for all that I wanted to see. White canvasses are overrated. They assume light to be the nature of the world. Black canvasses are much more pragmatic, assuming the best can only be achieved only with a certain combination of colors and strokes.

There was a rhythm to the pitter patter of the rain on the window. But it was a sad song, voiced by the winged-woman who flew to and fro in the dark clouds outside the window. Was she an angel, or something more devious? I wondered.

It all came to an end when there was a knock on the door, and Art entered.

The hours-long moment ended.

'Oh… thank goodness.'

'What do you mean?' I responded quietly, having realized that Martin had drifted into sleep.

'Well, we were under the impression that you had been fornicating for the last few hours.' He said this with all measure of sincerity; I was disgusted.

'Fornicating? Are you playing a joke?' I could not believe my ears.

'No.' Art looked down like a sad puppy.

'You are positively unbearable. Truly unbearable. Unbearable! Fornicating? Really? Given these circumstances? How idiotic one must to assume fornication in this situation. My God… and who is we?' I was once again quite irritated.

Art gestured for me to enter the hallway to avoid disturbing Martin. At least he was decent in this way. So I followed him into the hall, and sitting in front of me was none other than Hannah Herrman, who appeared more jovial than one would expect, given how I had torn at her like a rabid dog only hours before. She smiled—dammit—that smile! I could not escape it; it was positively wonderful.

She spoke: 'Virginia, I want to apolog...'

'No,' I responded. 'It is I who should apologize. I was made aware that any discreteness I tried to act with was highly ineffective.' She realized at once what I meant, as I gestured towards the bedroom. 'We spoke, and it would seem that, as weak as he is, Marty agrees with you, much to my own sadness.'

'In difficult times, there is little more we can do than pray that simple solutions present themselves.' She spoke candidly, which I appreciated now more than ever. 'So we shall fight our way.'

'May I ask what you mean by we?' I said. 'What interest do you have in helping our poor and pitiful souls?'

'Your poor and pitiful souls are not so poor and pitiful. If anything, they are stronger than many people. It takes a great deal of courage to accept the truth of a situation, especially when they are as complex and interconnected as the one we face now. I am a recorder of the facts and of the truth. I am also not one to back down from a giant. More than I can testify to that.' This comment visibly perplexed me, so she clarified, motioning towards Art. 'It would seem that by a strange and simply coincidental string of events, there are connections between us in ways more than one.' Another smile.

'Do you mean to say that the two of you have met before?' I asked.

'Yes, that's an appropriate way to phrase it.' Art let out a soft, guttural chuckle.

# XVIII

## DIARY OF VIRGINIA KELLY

*June 22nd*—And so it was today that Marty regained enough strength that we could begin the battle which lay before us. By 9:00, he was walking again, though he was undoubtedly a much more gaunt version of himself. His face was thinner, as were his appendages. And while there was no visible limp in his stride, it was weak. His demeanor was serious, but his spirits were high.

Art and Hannah had taken the liberty of letting us be to ourselves the previous evening, and while there was no question in my mind that fornication occurred, it seemed like a good opportunity for the two catch up. They spoke vaguely of some history and seemed to have a fairly apt understanding of one another, but I was clueless as to what precisely transpired between them. Unlike my usual hunger for secrets to be uncovered, the previous evening had taken a toll on my mind, and I was not in the mood to prod and probe, so I let them be.

They arrived at the hospital around 8:00, with a western-bound train schedule Marty had requested the previous evening, in the event that he feel well enough to travel today. For approximately an hour, Hannah, Art, and I stood around Marty's bed, discussing how we might best position our sling to down the giant.

Marty explained to us the extent of his work: 'The town of Paradiso, as I was told in a letter with my instructions, is the town which I have been asked to... amend. I have looked at the map, and it is not on any well-known rail lines. It is a morning's train ride north of Lake Tahoe. There are old rail lines there used by bootleggers to avoid the main junctures, where militant prohibitionists lie in wait.'

Art asked: 'So what do you mean to say? Won't simply going to this town and doing the Aesterna's bidding appease them all the more? Where is the fight, where is the battle?'

Marty took time to compose his response. 'They will be coming to inspect my work at the end of this week. They will stay in their house in the woods, which, although it is not too close to Paradiso, is within a reasonable distance. And there we will strike, cutting them as the bow to us on their knees, showing us their wrists destined to be bound.'

'Martin, do you need to be so blunt? Don't times like these call for moral restraint?' I asked.

'My dear... all is fair in love and war. But for the present, I shall do my best to exercise restraint.' There was silence as we all pondered this reality.

'So should we then leave as soon as possible? Perhaps

we can get to Reno by this evening if we go now?' Hannah asked.

'No, there is certainly not enough time. Only the unwise rush into things. Anyone with some semblance of knowledge waits for the unwise to realize their error—instead of for the wise to realize the unwise's error, which is an error in and of itself, then goes oneself, so that all possible errors have already been made. We will leave tonight, on the... 9:00 train. If I am right, then we will arrive in Reno on the morning of the... twenty-fourth. This will give us ample time to lay our trap and lie in wait. A matinee, anyone?'

'The Cabinet of Dr. Caligari is playing at the theater near the center of town...' I suggested.

'My dear, I am afraid that I am in far too weak a state to have a plot of that magnitude with horrific sounds thrust onto me.'

'What about the orchestra?' Hannah suggested. 'Wagner is being played this evening at 4:00... Wouldn't this leave us with enough time to catch the train?'

'Ah, yes! The orchestra. How wonderful that would be... and Wagner... fantastic. So it is settled.'


So by some odd sequence of events, we found ourselves sitting in the middle of the audience, underdressed compared to the hordes of pagans and patrons around us. The room began dark, but it was not too long before Wagner lit up the room. This particular selection, Die Walküre, had an unusually profound impact on the audience, which waved its arms and occasionally cried out, as if a totally encapsulating pastor spoke before them. The third movement especially seemed almost like a battle hymn. Its broad voice resonated deeply within me, but I could not discern whether the music was indicative of some great revelation to come, or if it was an epic which ended in death... Perhaps, I thought, I ought to learn a bit more about the Valkyries and their resounding ride. At the present, I believe them to be some great force of good—God's soldiers ready protect the pathétique life on earth. I pray my understanding is correct, as naive as it may be. The whole thing seemed very ominous.

When the show came to a close, we were the first out of the hall, with the train's departure at the forefront of our minds. We hailed a sizable car and squeezed ourselves into its back seats. The train station was not far, we were told—only twenty or so minutes away.

As we drove, we first passed a graveyard adjacent, but somehow hidden, to the orchestra hall. The grounds of the yard were covered in tombstones, packed quite close to one another. At the center of it all was a large maple tree. It was still a fiery red, despite it being June. This perplexed me. Nearby, a group of mourners stood, dressed in black, over an open grave.

'Marty, see those mourners? Wouldn't you hate to stand there as they are? In plain view of everyone who passes by? Don't you think that you'd like some privacy?'

'I suppose so. I'm not too inclined to care what others think of my grave. Quite frankly, if nine people love me enough to attend my burial, I think that I would be quite grateful. If even one person chose to attend my burial I think I would be quite grateful. That is the struggle with dying, after all. Those who show up to your burial are the only ones who really care about you. And you cannot even know who they are... because you are dead. I suppose there is the ecclesiastical view that one can watch over their own burial from 'above,' wherever that is, but even then, to watch your own burial seems quite paradoxical. I would imagine that those who move upwards after death need not hope that others attend their burial. Presumably they have done enough in the mortal realm to curry enough genuine favor so that at least one individual truly loves them. I suspect that most people who are dead and go... well... the opposite direction, are in the opposite situation— hoping that others attend their burials, I mean. Only the evil-doers in this life must cling to hope that they are in purgatory when they are buried, so that the decider of fate might take the number of people at one's burial into account. And I believe that nine is a respectable number of people at a burial. I would be more than happy if nine people took the time to stand over my body, while I am withering away in hell. Maybe that is the chance I speak of... but then I am just one of the people, I have postulated, who hopes that the quantity of mourners be a measure of good will in life. I suppose then that I should not care how many individuals stand over my grave when the time comes. Ah, but if I don't care, than how can I possibly have done anything worth remembering. I suppose I should possibly hope that some come to my burial. Ah but... it is quite paradoxical. Either way, I suppose the person being buried was quite respectable.'

Upon closer inspection, there were nine mourners, all women, all dressed from head to toe in black. Even the religious leader who stood at the head of them was a woman, but she was dressed in white. What heathens, I thought. There were several horses which stood around them, for what I assume were their pagan practices. There seemed to be a cloud over the small gathering—so much grief concentrated in one place... so much pain. No one in the car spoke, but everyone stared at the scene.

When we passed the graveyard, I realized that the clouds I imagined over the mourners had manifested in a particularly real fashion. Dark, practically black, clouds hung low over the city, wet with suffering. Rain began to fall when I leaned my head out of the car window and looked up. As we neared the train station, thunder and lightning simultaneously preached to us, as if to warn us of what was to come. The narrow columns of water looked like the bars of a heavenly prison cell, which we were about to escape with some degree of difficulty. I thought that perhaps it would have been better to remain in our cell, but quickly washed it away... after all, fate was my equal—or so I had decided.

As we got out of the car, the driver practically evicted us, in quite a violent manner. He parked, quite inconveniently, a good ways away from the entrance to the station. He remained in his seat, warmed by the car's engine, while the four of us stood in the rain, fussing with the back of the car, trying to open the trunk. When we did so at last, our luggage was soaked by a particularly harsh torrent of rain. We crossed the road, the four of us, with the rain beating us down and the wind slamming into our faces. Our voices were inaudible in the downpour, and we each had one hand on our hats to prevent them from being torn from our heads by the wind, and one hand guiding our luggage, of which there was no shortage.

We boarded the train and sat in our drenched clothes, chilled to our bones by nature's will. Perhaps it was a challenge. I was not ready to concede—not yet. Standing outside in the rain was also the last time I saw Hannah that day. She wore a red overcoat, though in the final moments, standing under the clouds in the pouring rain, her blood red coat turned a soft maroon. She was also the only one smart enough to bring with her an umbrella—also red—which she held like a spear in her right hand, ready to slay all in her path. For that I respected her.

We made our way through the station. The squeaking of shoes practically drove me mad. It was like we were back on the farm of my youth, and pigs were running wild. And like Hannah's coat had significantly dulled, so had Martin's. The vibrant green had taken on an earthy color, similar to the trees during the split second when summer and autumn meet, and duel for control of the scenery. The color lessened the size of his face quite substantially.

As sad as it was, he looked like death. That is not to say that he could not smile, or that he was not capable of being happy, but all his emotions were presented through an eschatological lens.

'Is there anything which I can do to make you cheer

up? Every way your face bends hints only of underlying pain. Is there no joviality left? I find it hard to believe that they could somehow rob you of your entire sense of sarcasm.' I chuckled, trying to draw a similar sound from him.

'Much to my disappointment, the world is bleaker now. They say ignorance is bliss—they're wrong. Ignorance is fucking heaven. We spend our lives preparing for the next, but fail to realize we can have it all now. All of it... now!' Marty spoke eagerly, as if he had had some great epiphany.

'My friend,' Art spoke with grave sincerity, 'you are beginning to sound like the pagans around you. I really think that you ought to reign yourself in and take back your comments. How can you bear to live a life where you do not know the truth? Shouldn't that be what we all aspire to? Living a knowledgeable and truthful life, in which we are aware of evil's presence, but not overly indulgent in it?'

'Art, my good Christian friend, think this: there is lots to know in the world. No doubt you can agree on this matter.' Art nodded. 'But, what do you do in the presence of all that knowledge?'

'What do you mean presence?' Art inquired. 'Knowledge is no physical entity, so how could it possibly be present? It exists only in our minds. There is no knowledge which floats in between our heads, that we can swipe down from the air and call our own. We must absorb knowledge with our senses. That is the only way we can obtain knowledge.'

'Sure, sure... but what if you did not even know that? What if you were not even aware of the presence of more knowledge than what lies beyond your head? To learn about that which is unknown is simply to uncover new problems, each of which requires, but lacks, a solution. Think about how truly stressful that must be. To know all the world's problems, but not solutions. To bear such knowledge would be the greatest burden of all—the worst hell known to man. Wherever you look, you would only be able to see problems... problems, problems, problems... no solutions... just problems... what kind of a life is that, my friend? What kind of a life are you living if the only thing which you strive for is knowledge of more problems than the human mind can fathom? There are problems which do not exist yet... they are present only in the future, when man has become so 'enlightened' that he is weighed down by the prospect of further discovery. It is a true predicament. That much I admit.'

'Gentlemen,' I said distastefully, 'you may enjoy your heady conversation, but it is quite difficult to follow, so I ask that, for now at least, you withhold further judgement, which I am sure there is no shortage of, until you two are in a space where your minds can run free without imposing on my well-being? Understood?'

'Of course,' they said in unison, one smiling, the other with his head hung low. Given the haste with which we purchased our tickets, no compartments were available, and we were lucky to find three seats in coach grouped so closely together without an occupant in the fourth, to make it square of course. And of the three of us, Art was perhaps the most lucky, as his overcoat was black to begin with. No amount

of rain could darken it. But perhaps it could be made more…
reflective.

So the three of sat there, and I began to compose this
entry. As of now, I decided that the fourth seat was for Hannah,
though I assumed she was somewhere else at the moment,
fighting her own giant.

# XIX

## CARTUS SUPPLICIUM OF EKATERINA AESTERNA

Initials: E.S.

    Supplicium date: June 18th

    Infraction: Late twice... June 8th & June 18th

Details: Lingua removed, collum snapped, trapezius severed, sternocleidomastoid severed, sternohyoid severed, 30% exsanguination

Disposal: Lake—deposited north

Notes: High perspiration, high respiration

## LETTER FROM O. AESTERNA TO E. AESTERNA
### Received June 22nd in Chicago

Ekaterina,

I will be returning from New York in a few days' time.

It is my hope that by the time of my return, the aircraft for which we placed an order several months ago will have arrived. It is my belief that within the next decade, air travel will become quite a part of high society, and we shall simply be ahead of the rest of the world—the way it ought to be.

I have heard little of our Californian problem, and as such assume that no news is good news. Quite unfortunately, we did lose another rather large shipment which was westward bound, despite a rather bloody exchange of ammunition. We lost several men, but the mountain people lost more. Some say spirit and zeal are of the utmost importance in matters of conflict and defense. I am of the mind that this is a fallacy. The only factor which must be taken into consideration is who can gun down the other with greater efficiency. Still, it does make me quite sad. Each of the men we killed had a mother, and each a wife; some had sisters, and some had brothers. And some of them were brothers and fathers and sons. I know that it may not burden your heart, but it surely does mine.

On a similar note, I must ask that you attempt to exercise greater restraint in your pursuits. I regret to say that although you might not follow the news too closely and we do not allow for any of it in the residence, I do follow it quite closely, and I am afraid that our confidence may have been betrayed by your negligence. It is especially worth noting that your poorly dumped bodies have been linked together, not only by their location, but their mutilation. In matters of the press, anything worth a headline is relegated to page two, so the human desire for the grotesque can be fulfilled. It is a shame.

But it is reality. And we have been thrust, not by name but by our—no your—actions, into a spotlight which we have aspired to keep off of ourselves for so long.

I also must share with you a particularly frightening dream which I had yesterday evening. Very early in the night, I felt a weight on my chest, but I was not conscious. In fact, I was quite unconscious. In this vision, I found myself in the center of a large castle, of the medieval sort. There were walls many times higher than I made of large stones with degrading grout. But there was a beautiful singing coming from a tower in the far corner of the castle. I felt as though I have heard these words before, but never in such a soft and seductive tone. It pulled me in, despite the fact my German is quite poor; the words were:

O Röschen rot,

Der Mensch liegt in grösster Not,

Der Mensch liegt in grösster Pein,

Je lieber möcht ich im Himmel sein.

Da kam ich auf einen breiten Weg,

Da kam ein Engelein und wollt mich abweisen,

Ach nein! Ich ließ mich nicht abweisen.

Ich bin von Gott und will wieder zu Gott,

Der liebe Gott wird mir ein Lichtchen geben,

Wird leuchten mir bis an das ewig selig Leben.

The whole thing was quite surreal. The courtyard in which I stood seldom obstructed the view of the tower. I stared up at the tower for several minutes before I took greater stock of my surroundings. And it was quite a grim scene:

There were three bodies hanging from an arch behind my head. All three were women: young and blonde. But their hair did not hang like their corpses. Instead, their hair flowed in the air, as if the bodies were suspended in water. The strands radiated outward, forming a corona and each of the three moons. Blood dripped down their dresses. I followed the blood down their gowns and onto the ground. Looking upon my own chilled feet, I realize they, too, were bare and doused in blood. This blood with the only hint of color in the drab scene. Everything else was either a stony grey, or an ethereal white.

Behind me a door swung open into the tower from which the singing emanated. I turned around to investigate who had so swiftly caused the door to open, but there was no one. But the singing drew me in. Leaving bloody footprints in my wake, I entered the dark void and took a staircase up many, many flights of stairs. The lyrics, which repeated again, and again, grew louder, but the sonorous appeal remained unchanged.

When I reached the top of the spiral, I pushed open a small door. Revealed to me in the tower was an image which even now I ponder. There were three women, each with long, straight, and golden hair. It hung down to their waists. And as I entered, they paid no attention to me, as if I were merely an invisible spectator, witnessing a cosmological sight too important for the maidens to take their attention off of. In the center of them was a spinning wheel. There were golden threads, each with a soft glow wound in the spool. And as the women spun the thread, they sang a most beautiful song.

For quite a long time, I stood in the door's archway, mesmerized by the women's craft. They spun the golden thread into a rope, which also glowed a soft, gold color. When the rope was finally quite long, the center of the three women began to fashion it into some shape, which I could not completely discern—her large hands hindered my view.

I was taken aback when the women with the limp rope rose to her feet, hands still obscuring my view, and the other two by her side turned to face me similarly. All three towered over me by several feet. The center woman's dress flowed even without a breeze coming through the slit in the tower. She began to approach me, and out of fear, I froze. I tried to run, but her gaze turned me to stone. When she stood only a feet from me, her soft hands pulled my own up to receive a gift. She drew the rope from her cloak and placed it in my hand. When I realized that the golden threads had been fashioned first into a golden rope, and then into a golden noose, my dream came to an end. I was overwhelmed by my vision. The fact alone that it culminated in my receiving a noose was enough. But as I slowly lost my senses and became unconscious in the unconscious realm, consequently becoming conscious in the conscious realm, the women's singing stopped, and they began to chant: 'She shall strike you down with the harm-bent sword. She shall strike you down with the harm-bent sword. She shall strike you down with the harm-bent sword...'

So then I lay awake, not wishing to sleep, defiant in my bed of grief. I remember it quite well. Dear Ekaterina, my hands are of your color, but I shame to wear a heart so white.

I am of the mind that the house will be ready upon our arrival at the end of the month, free of my nightmares, I hope, and that everything will be in place so that we might expand our operations—successfully—beyond their current borders. I will depart this city in two days' time.

O. Aesterna

LETTER FROM E. AESTERNA TO O. AESTERNA
Delivered to New York, June 27th—not received

Oz—

Your dream is particularly frightening, and so I would like to share one of mine. Though, much unlike your vision, my vision pertains precisely to the actions and events of the present. It goes as such.

In it, I am standing on the beach—the beach in California which we went to last summer. The one with the cold sand and the clouds. A salty breeze runs back and forth, as if to taunt us. It runs faster than I can. But you are not there— not by my side. I cannot even sense your presence nearby; I am by myself with the wind, and the sea and the clouds.

Much like your feet were stained with blood, so were my hands. But unlike in your vision, there were no hanging bodies or other source of the viscous liquid. It was just I, with my hands outstretched, dripping blood onto the earth. But the sand absorbed the blood.

Soon, the tide came in, and the water first lapped against my feet, freezing them to the bone, then later rose to my waist. Eventually, only my head was reliably above the water line. But just as I began to drown, the winds blew downward and forced the water back into the sea. As I regained my vision, I came to realize that the sea had turned red with the blood of my hands, and the white gown I was wearing had turned a similar, blood-red color.

It was a most interesting dream. And I am sure that there is a lesson worth pondering, as you say, in it somewhere. Unlike you, however, I do not have a mind which desires such greater meaning. I acquire it through other means. Which segues me quite well into my next point, being that you know, just as well as I, that I am a vampiric maniac.

Life is the only currency of value to me. And you know, just as well as I, that from a very young age (too young, some might say), this value was instilled in me by my crazed father. Some hoped that with age, my behaviors would die away... if I am not mistaken, you were one of them. It began as a sadistic ritual in my father's eyes, but I must admit that quite conversely, my clinical vampirism only grew into a... a necessary habit.

With all due respect, my loving husband, I will not stop my 'actionable pursuits.' It has become a part of me—they have become a part of me. When I sip the life force of others, I am made ecstatic, my own blood rushes about, and I am alive. Some primal instinct of mine is awoken—unlike anything else I know. Eventually, I will find the... elixir... which awakens me the most, and perhaps then I will be able to cease by actionable pursuits and settle down into domestic life. I think that you know quite well that this is my ultimate pursuit—for why else would we have all these artists staying in our house sucking on our livelihood? It is with their knowledgeable life force that our servants brew my mead. And it is because I drink it liberally that I am all the wiser. I realize that many often question my methods, but are they not genuine and effective, if even one person sees to it that they work? I surely am of the mind that it is so.

I will so much oblige your request in terms of greater discretion; though, I refuse to allow corpses on my property— high society simply does not allow for it. I wish you the best, but also realize that I stop for no one.

E. Aesterna

LETTER FROM THE CONDUCTOR TO HIS MOTHER
June 25th

Mother—

I write this to you as the train passes through Battle Mountain. I have had a series of stark observations which warrant sharing, and I see no one better to share with than you.

Chief among them is the migration of people, which has recently become quite a fascinating feat to me. Every day, I toil away on this train, punching tickets, serving drinks, calling out departure, and many things more. But while my duties remain constant, the lives of people change around me—constantly. There are some who are starting new lives, and some returning to old lives. Some people having simply left behind all they had for a chance to start anew—the ultimate risk one can take, which, on the whole, is quite admirable.

In the course of all my duties, I see many kinds of people. There are the rich and the poor, and the men and the women; there are the young and the old, the lost and the found. But all of them are on the train in search of something greater—something which they lack at the present. Perhaps it is a relative, or a house. But in many conversations, I have found that it is something greater. Some take the opportunity to search for purpose.

No one rides a train for fun. Fun is an arbitrary concept.

People ride trains to find something, whether it is physical, or metaphysical. I suppose that all things that could possibly be found are contained in one of the two sets.

Oftentimes, I find that those heading west do so for something new. After all, it is a newer land. The states are new, the land is new, the civility is new. But quite unfortunately, those traveling west for the 'new' are often the same individuals running from the east. Seldom does a man uproot his family on whim, or travel over three-thousand miles for pleasure. No. Those heading west are running, and as much as they might believe they are chasing, they are not. In fact, I surmise that the more people think they are chasing, the more they are really running; though, I am not qualified to speak about what they run from—I can only speculate about the vast number of things it could be.

But I suppose that the things which an individual seeks to find by riding the train are the same things which an individual seeks to hide—or leave behind—by riding the train.

You might recall that in my limited schooling in Denver, I took a quarter on theoretical cosmology. At the time, I could hardly decipher the meaning of the term, let alone the material. But in my profession, I have come to realize that there are many lonely hours, and I have taken to reading quite intensely in my spare time. One of my current favorites, though I cannot recall precisely from which faith it comes, tells of how the sun and moon are constantly chased by wolves. And though I am aware that—scientifically speaking—this is rubbish, to my occasionally wandering mind it makes perfect sense. Chiefly because everyone—without exception—has a wolf, or several, which chase them throughout life. In the morning, I sit towards the front of the train and watch the sun rise directly ahead, the wolf's gashing teeth snapping at it from below. Throughout my day, in quiet moments of reflection, I look up to the sun, and the wolf close behind—sometimes closer, sometimes farther. And then, as the day comes to a close, I sit in the rear and watch the sun plunge into the ground of the West, seizing the light it temporarily lends, first from the drifting, then from the rooted.

Every day I see people running—and I watch them run. They carry themselves in a way that is distinct from everyone else. They clutch what is theirs and envy what belongs to others. What a miserable life it must be. But then again, is it not the life which we all live? Perhaps my next note will be on a more cheerful subject. I can only hope so. But the days on the train are long and oftentimes seem endless, so perhaps my wolf has already caught up with me.

With love,
R.T.S.

## DIARY OF VIRGINIA KELLY

*June 23rd*—So our plan is formulated. And I shall document the discussion which led to its formulation in its totality here, so that its details may remain refined and precise.

Marty, credit due to him, did in fact time our departure quite well. We departed the Salt Lake on the evening of the twenty-second and arrived the night of the twenty-third in Reno, Nevada. The evening, after we reclined our seats and dried our clothes in the windows of the car, was rather pleasant. We played cards and ate ribs—essentially the only luxury which we were afforded during our journey. Martin also took the liberty of explaining to us, in perhaps greater detail than was necessary, the awful things which occurred around him in the House of Aesterna. There were many tears and embraces. But these were emotions I had already faced, and his anecdotes only added to my understanding. Despite the moist nature of the car from both the rain and our tears, we all slept quite well.

Quite early this morning when few others were awake, and the sun had hardly risen above the horizon, I felt a hand shaking me with a significant degree of hurry. I flipped onto my back and, after almost falling off my seat on the floor, opened my eyes to see Hannah leaning over above me, with her finger over her lips, gesturing for me not to speak.

She had quite some audacity entering the white-only coach car. I realized that she was committed to seeing our yet-to-be formed plan through, and I respected her for the bold move. Still in my sleeping gown, I collected myself and followed her into the lounge car, where, thankfully for us, no one was yet imbibing.

'What brings you here so early?' I asked her. 'You could get in quite some trouble if you were found to be sneaking through our car. Someone might think that you were trying to steal. There would be a fairly short-lived investigation, and you would quite quickly be sentenced—perhaps be forced off the train even.'

'First to address your concern—if people are so petty as to object to my presence on the basis that they assume I am a thief, then it is they who do not deserve to be on a train with me.' I liked this answer. 'And now to matters of real importance. While you are surely correct that I cannot be with you for too long, in a matter of hours, we will get off this train and be in a city which none of us are familiar with. Virginia, we need a plan. I realize that Martin and perhaps Art have the courage and perhaps the wherewithal to know that, but you need at least instigate the discussion of the formation of a plan.

If we lack a plan, then we are simply a horde of vagabonds in the mountains hoping that the chance to kill the Aesternas presents itself.'

'Hannah! Now who mentioned anything of killing them? I am a good Christian and can do no such thing.' I was truly appalled.

'Then I will kill them if you do not want to. That is okay, I understand.'

'No! I cannot participate in a plan which I believe even in the slightest will result in the death of another human form. I simply cannot.' Hannah sighed at this.

'Well, then I ask this of you. Do not change your view of me as a person. I have never killed another person, nor do I intend to kill another person in the near future—or the far future for that matter. It was merely a suggestion. I too had thought very little of it, and it only stems from my experience that...'

'That what? How can you ever justify taking another's life? It is simply unspeakable.'

Her voice rose and she continued to speak.

'...my experience that evil is relentless in all respects. And that so long as it exists, even in the slightest, it is more than capable of reproduction. So, it would follow—quite logically— that to stop the spread of evil, it cannot simply be imprisoned. So...,' she paused, encouraging me to answer. I would do no such thing, so Hannah answered her own question. 'So sometimes we must just... end it.'

'End it?'

'Yes.' She responded; though this time, she was slightly more dignified.

'No.'

Her head rolled back.

'Why?'

'Your logic is impenetrable, I admit. But reason cannot solve all the problems in the world, especially in cases of morality.' I spoke truthfully. I could not participate in a plan which would end in the death of another human being. It was simply against all of my principles.

'Virginia,' she stared into my eyes for slightly longer than a moment, 'take some time in here, and ponder. Just ponder. What are the true consequences if... well, you know. If hell is the worst of it, then perhaps the benefits outweigh the detriments. Just do me the favor of looking at the whole picture, will you?'

I would do no such thing, but out of respect for Hannah and her overt commitment, I obliged her. She, looking quite satisfied, returned first through my car, then back to the coach car from which she came. I stood in the lounge for several minutes. And though I could not see the sun rise, I saw the golden rays it cast on the Nevada desert, and I saw the shadow of the train in the center of it all.

After five minutes of pondering, not murder, but the scenery, I assumed sufficient time had passed that Hannah would have already returned to her seat several cars down, and thus would be unaware that I had returned to my own seat, despite having not pondered her ideas in the slightest. But as

I entered my own coach car, directly adjacent to the lounge, I saw the back of Hannah's flannel dress going through the opposite door. Several wild explanations ran through my head, but because both Art and Martin remained steadfastly asleep, they all entered through one ear and passed out the other with ease.

An hour or so later, the three of us gathered in the dining car for our breakfast. Over eggs and toast and sausage, we discussed trivial matters: the weather, our soaked clothing, avoided the matter of what to do once we arrived in Reno. It went on this way for quite some time until Martin, like Hannah had suggested, had the wherewithal to spur conversation on the matter.

'First,' he said, 'we must establish our goal. Unfortunately, Hannah is not here at the moment to give us her advice, but what are your thoughts?'

Art spoke next.

'I see no problem with killing them; I think it could be quite justified. It is after all what they did to others: an eye for an eye, a limb for a limb.'

'My gosh, you pagans!' I could hardly restrain myself. 'How can you call yourself Christians when you consent to murder?

'The Righteous will rejoice when he sees the vengeance; he will bathe his feet in the blood of the wicked.' Art responded quickly.

'How dare you twist the will of the Lord? I can hardly bear your presence!'

Martin then did his best to infuse reason into our discourse.

'So perhaps, we shall not execute them. Instead, capture? Can we all agree that capturing the Aesternas would make this operation well worth our time?'

'Yes.'

'Yes, I suppose so, though you may need to check with Hannah.'

'Very well, so then our goal is to capture them.' Martin glanced at Art with eyes wide open. Art nodded. So we were all in agreement.

'Then this is what we shall do. I consulted a map before I slept. We shall spend the night in Reno, perhaps enjoy the nightlife, where there are ample lights and plenty to do. Then it will be the twenty-forth. On the morning of the twenty-fourth, we will find ourselves to Paradiso. You two, and Hannah, will rest while I investigate the town. I must become familiar with the people who run it, so that they will be our allies in our quest to apprehend the Aesternas. It is likely that they despise the Aesternas as much as if not more than we. I have heard by way of the news there have repeatedly been gun fights in the town between locals and bootlegger mercenaries. We will take advantage of this. Then, on the twenty-fifth, we and a band of fighters from the town will sneak through the woods late at night and lie silently. The Aesternas will soon after arrive. If I am not mistaken, they will be flying a new airplane into a nearby field which is being prepared specifically for them. They will then arrive at their house, and we will apprehend them—

capture them. Yes?'

'Sounds quite well to me,' I said.

'Yes, a great plan.' Art responded, maintaining eye contact with Martin.

We spent the remainder of the time on the train packing our bags. Nature surely smiled upon us that day. The weather was quite pleasant; though, the altitude was somewhat sickening. There were moments of light-headedness, but ample hydration kept them at bay.

'Marty,' I asked in a quiet moment, 'will you promise me one thing?'

'Likely, but I cannot do so for certain, unless you tell me what it is which I am promising you.'

'I ask, quite simply, that you not knowingly kill another human. I simply cannot stand the thought of you—or Art or Hannah or anyone who I care deeply about—willingly taking another's life.' He paused for a moment, leading me almost to believe that he might not promise. That would certainly crush me more than anything else he tell me, or do.

'Certainly, I can promise you that.'

Relief.

The train pulled in to the Reno platform earlier than we expected, sometime around noon. The mountain air was particularly refreshing. The station itself was surrounded by pine trees, the scent of which was obscured only by smog emerging from the train. I do concede, however, that upon further inspection, it was quite an unlawful place. There were hooligans in every direction, and despite prohibition at the federal level, drunks were everywhere in the streets. Perhaps these were the dissident descendants of gold miners from the bygone century. I had heard of them, trying still to stake their claim in their father or grandfather's name, maybe even strike it rich.

None of them succeeded. Not the one, or so I heard.

Hannah and I reunited quickly after disembarking the train. No one offered to carry her luggage. How rude of them, I thought. So she came barreling towards me with her suitcases, still wearing her blood-red coat. Evidently it had dried out some bit and was restored to its original color.

Unlike in the East, where at least some individuals were respectfully, and the Rocky Mountains, where all the pagans were too pacifistic to insult another human, the rapscallions of the West shot Hannah nasty looks—because of her being colored, I assume. If it was because she was a woman, then I too would be assaulted by hatred. But I was not. Only destitute singles threw glances my way. Many went out of their way to make Hannah Herrman feel unwelcome; there were a few other colored people in Reno at the time, but they all worked relatively menial jobs and kept their eyes to the road. I hope they have dreams. To labor without a dream is the ultimate toil.

We walked through town and observed the life around us. At the present, all the able-bodied men were felling lumber in the nearby woods, or brewing in their basements, so the streets were free of genuine economic determination. Only the lowlifes and drunks wandered about. And for the most part, the women stayed hidden. There was one particularly beautifully dressed woman who sat on the deck of a saloon and scowled at us from under her large sunhat, which radiated outwards from her head. A blue ribbon which crossed under her chin and slightly touched her throat kept the hat in place. She also wore a dress, unlike the other women in the area, who wore all variety of clothes, but not dresses. It was simply not the appropriate weather for a long dress.

We made our way down a main avenue to the inn at which we would take up residence for the night. It was a cozy place, but apparently quite empty at the time. Refusing to allow Hannah to share a room with Art, on the grounds of both their relative gender relation status and her color, we took up in three rooms: one for Hannah (a small dingy thing on the top floor in the corner), one for Art, and one for Martin and me (a larger room, quite well furnished with ample local touches—this, I appreciated as a woman of taste). For several hours, we lounged in our rooms. Hannah and I devoured our literature, while Martin resumed his careful cartography, for which he had absolutely no formal training; I often find that men do this: they take to fields and practices which they are simply not supposed to in life and consequently mess up a great deal of things. Also, I have not the slightest clue how Art occupied his time. I was yet to uncover what he appreciated in life; though, I am sure it is either equally as complex or equally as vain as either reading literature or making maps, respectively.

When at last, after our long day of travel, we found ourselves sitting at the table, we joined our hands in prayer. This was at Art's request; though he had been of the mind that

225

killing the Aesternas was acceptable, he was a profoundly holy man and valued his being close to the Lord. He spoke:

'Dear God, may You be merciful. As our minds are challenged in the days to come, and we face impossible tasks, may You understand that there is error in our decisions. But that within all of our error, we try our best in Your name. We shall weigh the scales of justice to the best of our knowledge, but when it is merely a feather which makes the ultimate difference, we ask that You be by our side. Many tribulations You have shown us through, and there are many more to come. In the many years we have been blessed with, never will we face such a challenge as what tomorrow, the day after, and the day following hold. In Your name, I pray for all the scared children, great and small. When breath we have not, when energy we have not, no warmth, nor motion, no healthy looks; I pray You are by our sides. And in Your name: great glory we have gained if though we die now or tomorrow or soon after; no man survives a single dusk beyond Your decree; Amen.'

It was a particularly introspective prayer. And it forced me to consider the possibility that the others had accepted some undue fate which I was still unaware of. I felt ousted despite the inclusive nature of this particular grace.

The waitress approached us. She wore a thin white dress with a black apron. Her red hair was tied tightly back in a large and voluptuous bun behind her head. She spoke musically, but what began a nice melody turned into cacophony: 'Due to a lack of business as of recently, we only can offer you two things this evening, beef and lamb. If I could advise to ladies and gentlemen, the beef is, well, older than it perhaps should be. The lamb, however, is quite excellent. So what will it be?' The others were shaken by the kind woman's advice.

'Lamb.'

'Lamb.'

'Better be the lamb.'

'Beef.'

'Virginia,' Martin whispered, 'did you not just hear this kind woman's warning about the beef?'

I rose my hand to his face with grave sincerity.

'Marty—I am not one for the lamb.'

'But...'

'The beef! Please...' This shut him up. If it did, I do not think I would know what to do. We all quietly consumed our dinner, largely minding only our plates and business. Seldom did we probe one another's business, as had previously been done while trying to discern whether the individuals seated around the table would be of the sort willing to commit murder. Maybe it was only I who was thinking this in particular.

The meal came to an end, and I was the first to retire. After addressing the appropriate measure of hygiene—this inn was recently constructed and had a tub, with a hot water machine, so that I could take my weekly warm bath. I bathed for some fifteen minutes, conjuring suds and rinsing them away. By the time I was done, I was quite reluctant to exit the tub. In the last few moments, I had grown quite fond of the warm water. Standing upright, the cold air clung to the naked wetness of my skin. The only relief was the towel. After drying and dressing in my gown, I found the thin slip between the bedding to be my small temporary haven. One can work any job in the world as long as they have good bedding. It is, after all, the rejuvenator of life.

But for the longest time, Martin did not enter the room. And the common area, only a few tens of yards away from where I lay in bed, produced no sounds. I called out to Martin: no response. Another call: no response. This was odd, but I accepted that he had many fascinations, and as long as there was no flippant fornication involved, who was I to object to his will.

So I set down my novel and began to compose this entry. The events of the day were so clear, but the morals could not have hidden more subtlety.


NOTE I, three hours later—I write this only by the slight light of my bedside candle. Some hour after I extinguished the light from my room hoping that Martin would soon waltz back in, he did so. But instead of a waltz, it was some wild dance, and my mind spun like the Danse Macabre, the likes of which I did not know. He bumped into tables and knocked over the local shrubbery. I even could hear him vomit into the washtub. It was a most disheartening sound. I can only hope that it was something which he ate. Perhaps I had been ultimately correct in my choice of avoiding lamb. Maybe Art and Hannah were also up to their waists in vomit from the night's meal. There were potatoes and vegetables. And for dessert, there were fruits and cream and chocolate. In hindsight, any number of things could have upset his stomach. How I was ever supposed to diagnose him, I do not know.

And so out of concern for Martin as he lay next to me, sleeping above the bedding entirely, I compose this miniature piece.

NOTE II—I have sat in the darkness for just a moment, and in doing so, had a sudden realization, so I once again sparked a light to add my thoughts to my diary: I have now travelled into every world within this country's land (the east and middle and west). And I surmise that the West is where men die down to from hell... either that or the tenth circle.

# XXI

## DIARY OF VIRGINIA KELLY

*June 24th*—It was quite early this morning when I found myself alone in the hotel room. Art, Martin, and Hannah had disappeared, and the only notice I had which prevented me from summoning authorities to the scene of a kidnapping with a note from Martin was scrawled on a napkin in slanted handwriting. It read:

Va—be back in a few hours. We all have business to tend to for the plan. Hope you slept well. Please don't get into trouble. With love, MT.

I cannot help but think that to some degree I was being swindled. I, too, was a valuable part of this group, or so I thought. To be dismissed in such a rudimentary manner as not performing some necessary duty was undoubtedly a slap to the face. The whole thing was only compounded by my fear that the 'plan,' which grew more ominous by the moment, was not fully within my view. The thought that I was excluded certainly crossed my mind. But I think that it is important not to rush to judgement in such matters. I trust Martin, very much so. He would only lie to me if it was quite a good reason, and my primary concern—willful manslaughter—had already been put to rest by his word. The only part which stung was that I, the simple minority, was excluded.

Touché to the asses!

I decided to go about my day as I saw fit. And it is they who were willfully excluded from my fun. After a hearty meal, I set out on my day's business. The present day was much similar to the previous, the same cool mountain air and piney scent. It almost had a toasty tinge like the breakfast in the country. The sun was bright, and before it rose to its fullest high, it sat on the horizon and forced the buildings in front of it into silhouettes.

The main street was long. It was paved, but with ample dirt on its surface. There were automobiles, but not too many, and those that did roam the streets were certainly not of the nicer variety.

The facades of the buildings appeared relatively well kept, but antiquated nonetheless. There was lots of brick and concrete boxes, and the little architectural interest that did populate the city was not too impressive itself. In all of these ways, I did prefer the larger cities, of greater intrigue. What the town lacked, however, was largely compensated for by the nature, which the cities would only be able to truly experience in the event of an apocalypse, or if they were built again from scratch. This small town was surrounded by nature—lots of it. The air—which I have mentioned many times already—is much more clean than in the squares or on the pavement in urban areas. It is good for the soul, I suspect, to periodically be exposed to clean air, so that the badness within can permeate outwards—a catharsis of sorts. And there is much more genuinely wild life. When I sit in parks, only pigeons take the time to visit, and they are not too pleasant when they do so. But in the little town, there is ample life swirling around me like an all-encompassing wind.

Since it was a Friday morning, the streets were slightly more crowded. There were more women going about their business. Friday mornings, it would seem are a popular time for women to gather and play bridge; the wealthier among them at least. The time at which I walked through the street also lent itself well to observing the tail of local laborers migrating to their jobs for the day. Many of them wore beards. Some wore overalls. All looked tired.

I had a most curious interaction with one of the men as he walked towards the forest and dropped a cloth—some kerchief, I assume.

'Excuse me, sir...' This did not catch his attention; logically, I spoke louder. 'Sir... Sir!' The man swirled around on his right foot, with his left dragging in the dust, kicking it up with notable success. 'I believe you dropped your kerchief.' I was some ten yards from it, while he was only ten or so feet away. He made silent eye contact with me for just enough time for a slight discomfort to set in. He limped back over to the spot where he dropped the kerchief and bent down, putting his left hand behind his left knee to prevent it from collapsing beneath him.

'Much obliged, ma'am. You are not from around here, are you?' He stood, body and head cockeyed, both leaning to the right.

'No, I'm afraid I am not. I arrived last night on the western bound Streamliner.'

'May I inquire about what your business is here? It is not every day that we are blessed with the presence of the bourgeoisie in our... forest grotto.'

'Unfortunately, I am just passing through and will be gone before the day is out. But the mannerisms of the people here are quite interesting.'

'I must agree, ma'am. We are a town of the toilers and toiled, put here by destiny. There is no way to avoid it. Association with this place carries certain... connotations which you can never successfully escape.'

'If I may ask, sir, you speak with intelligence. You talk of the bourgeoisie and the toilers and the toiled and fate. How come you are a...'

'A worker, ma'am; tried and true...'

'How come you, a... worker... speak so wisely?'

'As I said, there are certain connotations one cannot escape when they are associated with such a lawless place, and I am not one to live a lie. I suppose that, in theory, I could rechristen and present myself to the civilized world, but I then run the risk of having the elder of my identities unveiled to much ruin, more so than I have now. It's not a situation which

I want to become engrossed in.'

'I suppose I can respect that initiative. But how can you sequester your mind and perform such menial physical tasks? Don't you have much to share with the world?'

'Not anything which I have not already shared with myself.' He finished this sentence with a smile and a pause. He continued: 'We all are, in essence, shaped by the blood and bones of the people before us into man-shaped molds. Why should it make a difference who I share my thoughts with?'

'Wouldn't the people of society appreciate what you have to say?'

'It's a real possibility. But I have tried, and failed. There is no point in imposing one's thoughts onto others who so willingly admit that they would never accept such thoughts.'

'So I suppose you are then bound to silence for life... You are okay with this?'

'Aren't I talking with you now? This is certainly not silence. I think you'd agree.'

'Yes, but...'

'You, ma'am,' he paused, gently waiving his hand to request my momentary silence, 'are willing to listen to my thoughts. And if you share them with others who are willing to listen, then perhaps there is a greater chance they will be heard. In matters of persuasion, substance is irrelevant and presentation is paramount. I am of the mind that, after all, we humans are only faces for our ideas, the medium through which our ideas interact with the world.'

'You are softly insightful for a laborer. What is your

specific role in the local economy?'

'A blacksmith, ma'am, but at present, I am heading to the forest to collect wood for my fires. Healthy fires only burn when something is destroyed in ample quantities.' Another long pause. 'I have much appreciated your time, but I am afraid that I must be on my way. Such flammables do not collect themselves.' He tipped his dusty hat in my direction and limped off towards the forest. It was not long until he was out of sight, and I was once again alone in the streets of the dirty little city.

Alone, I continued to wander down the street past all manner of shops: cobblers and leatherworkers, and bakeries and fudge shops; there were tailors and farriers, but for all that I saw, there was not one metallurgy building. The long street ended at a rectangular building, quite modern in nature. It was—boxy… and signage indicated it was the city hall. I walked around to the front and saw the large doors propped open. More signage—this time a large banner with red lettering—read: COMMUNITY FORUM—ALL WELCOME. Curious to further investigate the local way of life, I entered the building. There was a small vestibule, which even my head could touch the top of, which gave way to a larger foyer. Doors were open which I observed, from the foyer, led to an auditorium. An attendant stood to the right of the entrance.

'May I ask what the current subject of discourse is?' He looked at me with starry eyes. I rephrased: 'What are the gentlemen talking about? I intend to listen.'

'Oh… um… right… something to do with temperance or prohibition, or whatever the shoe-lickers call it… maybe.

But I am supposed to inform you that women are discouraged from entering.'

'On what grounds?' I was taken aback by this insinuation.'

'This is government, madam.'

'Preposterous.'

'It's just not... your place.'

'You should know that your sign so dutifully says all welcome. Am I not one of all?'

'Madam...' The troll tried to reassure me. No such thing would take place.

'Perhaps your little hick town has forgotten that women achieved suffrage less than a decade ago.' This comment increased tensions noticeably to the point of utter silence. Both of our chins were raised—ready for battle. But my chin was higher. I picked myself up from the battle field and waltzed past him into the auditorium. Perhaps these trolls could use a woman's perspective.

But there were no women. Instead it was all men, and teenagers (male), not one of whom was speaking with a level head. Democracy at its finest, I thought. Not deterred by the vehement masculinity around me, I took a seat in the middle of the auditorium, somehow unnoticed by the vast majority of people. Those who did notice me paid little attention. I observed the debate below. It would seem that the city officials were dueling with angry town people—of the more agrarian, rural, forested nature; it took me a moment to realize the topic of debate. The whole thing was practically a play beginning in medias res:

'The city shouldn't enforce its goddam shoe-licker laws on us! I'll shoot the bastards before they touch my fucking door knob!'

'Mr. Wild, it is the Constitution you are insulting! We are a country of common law, and to think that you are exempt from an amendment is outrageous.'

'What is outrageous is that we can't keep that which is ours! If want to make shine then it is ours... There ain't nothing you can do about it.' This comment incited a roar of applause from all around the room, as all the forest dwellers yelled their two cents—the last of the few cents they had.

'Perhaps you cannot get it through your mind, but it is the same set of rules that lets you have your gun which prevents you from making your moonshine! You must see the hypocrisy of your actions. You simply cannot elect to follow the rules which you like and disregard those you don't. It's un-American! Treason to the highest degree!'

'No! You know what's treason? It's taking our property. For your own goddam enjoyment. All you shoe-lickers probably just sit in your offices and get drunk off our stuff! We won't have it!'

'That is absurd!'

'Prove it! Show us our shine which you stole! Our property which you put your greedy hands on!' This left the official quite without words, as he could not comply with the troll's near-sighted request—speaking of which, all the forest people resembled trolls: they were short, fat, and dressed like...

trolls, for lack a better word.

Not before long, the yelling became quite repetitive, as the novel brains of the trolls failed to formulate arguments which went beyond their own materialistic desire. I excused myself from the forum with great politeness.

In hindsight, the whole scene upset me greatly. On one hand, the people advocated for their interests, as short-sighted as their interests were. Despite the fact I am a well-schooled woman, I am still yet to have a formalized opinion of democracy. Democracy is irony, and irony is democracy. The people were jousting for their rights, but they so clearly erred in their logic. How can important decisions be left to such impulsive people? I cannot imagine my fate in their hands. I suppose this is why we have separation of church and state, so that our fate is not solely in the hands of the government—only if this happened, I think, would I feel truly violated.

If the ultimate aim of democracy is peace, it surely did not accomplish that in the previous hours. If the ultimate aim of democracy is stability, it surely did not accomplish that either. If the ultimate aim of democracy is safety, the last few hours have done the exact opposite. What good has it done us? But then again, if the people could not speak with their lips, perhaps they would speak with their arms. Quite honestly, I much prefer the former to the latter.

My self-guided tour of the primary avenue came to a conclusion at the base of a statue of a mustached man. He bore a pickax in his right hand and leaned on it with a contrapposto stance. Disappointed by the sight which I had just witnessed, I cared not to read the plaque. The man's stance in and of itself conveyed to me the complete atmosphere of the town.

The remainder of the day was spent reading literature—fine literature. And it was a significant relief to once again be immersed in a world where outcomes, even if unknown, have undoubtedly already been determined. I hope the others are loathing their pursuits as much as I.


## LOG OF ARTHUR LAWRENCE


*June 24th*—After a slight re-assignment of roles to accommodate discretion, Marty dispatched me to convene with the mountain people and secure their aid in our endeavors. In speaking with the innkeeper, she advised me as to speak with one of the more prominent of the mountain people, and gave me directions to the family's cabin accordingly. Setting off early in the morning, an hour or so before the sun rose, I took to my feet through the woods.

The trees were dense, but the air crisp. Light seldom broke through the canopy, but when it did, it can down in firm and straight rays and cast spotlights on morsels of nature—a beautiful thing it was.

There were little brooks and foliage. Ground squirrels darted back and forth on the ground, up and down trees. One in particular which I watched emerged from the hole at the base of a tree and climbed straight towards the sun. When it was at last out of view, the light from above was momentarily eclipsed by a large bird—an eagle, I assume; I have always wanted to see an eagle, so when a large raptor passes overhead, I simply assume it is an eagle. In this way, I have seen an eagle many times.

The ground was dense with plants, and many times I nearly tripped, but the dense ground eventually opened into a large clearing, from which a serene pond was visible in the distance. It was on the other side of this pond which the innkeeper advised me that I would be able to find the woman, who she referred to as the 'matriarch of the woods.' At the time the innkeeper relayed to me her title, I could hardly keep from laughing. But after interacting with the woman for several minutes, I was taken aback.

When I approached the shore of the pond, which was some hundred yards across, I could make out a small cabin opposite where I stood. The newly risen sun cast its rays onto the body, where bright and thick vapor rose from its reflective surface. There was a faint column of smoke which rose up from the woods below, behind the pond's vapors, that I could hardly make out.

Remaining on the beach, I half circumnavigated the pond. When I came to the little cabin, I was mesmerized by the variety of activities which were simultaneously taking place. What first struck me was a large dog—dare I say wolf—chained to a tree several paces detached from the house. Its teeth—no, fangs—were noticeably sizable, but unlike most wolves one encounters, which snap at newcomers and guests, this particular wolf slept quite soundly, as if comforted by having recently completed a task with the utmost success. Some ways away beside the wolf was a small graveyard, in which a child danced around, plucking his lute. As he plucked, he cast seeds about for the scarlet-red chickens to consume. When I appeared, the chickens looked at me and cocked their heads as chickens do. Engrossed in his music, however, the child continued to dance. A short distance away, but submerged all the deeper into the woods were a group of young women, sitting in a circle weaving some sort of cloth. They were not children, but were young-creatures, beautiful southern ladies, spinning white linen. Not one of them took notice of me.

Included in my observations was a clearer view of the cabin. It was large and fairly well-built for a handcrafted residence. There were windows cut out of the frame periodically along its side, and a second level above the part of the house which stuck further into the woods.

As I took it all in, this peculiar way of life, I do not think I had ever been more frightened as when a large door, which I had not noticed because of the dark continuity of the log exterior, swung open. From the opening emerged the largest woman whose presence I had ever graced. She stood easily two feet more than I, and much unlike other women of the era, held a shotgun (aimed at me) with more comfort than any man I knew. She was dressed, based on civil society's standards, in rags.

'What are you doing here?' She gripped the muzzle tightly; her knuckles turned white as the blood was squeezed out of them.

'I am here only to seek your assistance… but I ask that you put your gun down! Nothing civil can be done with arms in question.' I blocked my face with my hands—as if it would protect in the event the woman concluded I was not fit for her presence.

'What do you want?' The gun dropped slightly but her expression soured.

'Your help!'

'How can you want my help? I can't be any help—not to anybody.'

'But I think you can. The old keeper at the Diamond Hotel suggested that you have influence over all the people who live throughout the woods.'

'She may be correct about that, but I don't see how that can be of service to you, unless you're trying to… raise an army.' Provoked by her phrase, she raised the gun again to point at my chest, gripping it tightly. 'No army solicitors welcome here! Get out before you try to convert us into your foot soldiers.'

'Ma'am, I intend to do no such thing.'

'Then are you one of the shoe-lickers here for our shine? 'Cause we're not giving it up! You'll have to pry it out of our cold, dead hands.'

'No! The opposite!'

'So you intend to sell us shine? Plenty of 'ootleggers have already tried that, and there is a forest of bodies which tells how that sad story ends. So your reason better be quite unique in its nature.'

'Strangely it is a combination, to some degree of all the above.'

'You mean to say that you're an 'ootlegger here to steal our shine and enlist us in some phony army to fight the shoe-lickers?'

'Might I explain?' By now, I felt as I was bargaining for my life.

'You'd better do so quickly! We got our little heaven out here where we do our work and keep to ourselves. No one quite appreciates trespassers all too much.' As if I could not discern that from the present situation.

'I seek to enlist help—not soldiers—to kill bootleggers, and I don't see why you could not materially benefit from such a bargain.'

'You want our help to kill bootleggers?'

'Yes.'

'Then you must be the gov'ment!' Again, the gun was drawn up to my chest.

'No!'

'Then why you want to kill 'ootleggers? You're 'robly doing pretty well off 'cause of them.'

'No! Not everyone consumes alcohol of their own free will—and the bootlegger, they hurt people.'

'Who doesn't 'urt people? I bet you 'urted some people in your day.'

After more candid speech, tensions were relaxed and we entered into frank conversation. The matriarch's name— or the title by which she was addressed— was Mam Hulda.

The former portion of the name, I assume, was derived from some woodland combination of 'ma'am' and 'mother,' but the latter portion left me quite dumbfounded. I learned, also, that the three woman who spun linen and the boy who danced on the graves with his lute were her children. Their names, forest amalgamations similar to their mother's, were so obscure that my memory cannot recall them.

When I spoke of my proposition to Mam, she agreed with reluctance, and knew of the small town of Paradiso, of which I spoke.

'I have heard many stories of the place, all of which are quite conflicting. Some describe it as a small haven. There is a spring and lots of children who run around the streets—until the bullets fly. The trains arrive, and everything goes to hell. The guns come out and the lives float away; a true tragedy. But I admit that we (the forest people) are worse off because of the violence. We get our liquor, but the souls that have been lost ain't worth the shine. So if you, Arthur, can promise me that no more souls will wither away through the trees because on what you're dreamin' up, floatin' up like the steam and the 'moke, then I am more than sure that you can find 'elp in us.'

I thanked the Mam for her time, and, without realizing she was illiterate, wrote down the details, of when and where to meet us in Paradiso. Thankfully, just before I departed, I verbalized the instructions, which seemed to have stuck.

I set off back towards the Diamond Hotel. The sun was at its peak, and cast its light through the entire forest with its more prominent position in the sky. Given the later time, my walk back towards town cast light on the timber fellers in the distance, who took no notice in me, beyond the simple: 'Watch for fallin' trees!'

I spent the remainder of the day examining the town. Martin already left for Paradiso, to assess the atmosphere of the town and learn the details of the Aesterna's chalet and arrival, so I was left that evening to dine with Hannah and Virginia. Only when such a prominent member of a party is gone does one realize the impact of their conversation. The meal was largely silent, but we all spoke of our doings for the day. Hannah, it turned out, had been fulfilling her role as an investigator and was collecting interviews from the people. She spoke of a town hall she briefly entered, in which a couple of men, after being persuaded to talk to Hannah despite their apparent prejudice against her, spoke violently of their desire to 'keep his stake of the shine.' Virginia was especially flustered by this comment. She seemed quite shaken by the subtle contents of the little city.

# XXII

## DIARY OF HANNAH HERRMAN

*June 25th*—Never have I been more confused, sad, happy, and scared—simultaneously. Many say the night hides people and conceals their image. But anyone who has ever played the game of hide-and-go-seek must realize that being hidden allows one a unique perspective on things. It is often only when one is hidden that secrets reveal themselves.

The morning was quite eventful. We packed our bags and bought a wagon to Paradiso. The forest, though dark, was quite nice. It did not conceal our identities as well as the night, but nature did well to partially eclipse our faces. The horses were musty, and the road, if it can be called a road, was bumpy. Large boulders stood in our way, and Art had to periodically help the driver move fallen trees from the path. At one of these junctures, Virginia took the opportunity to question me; she had, after all, been looking quite uneasy for the greater part of that day.

'Do you think that Martin is well? I mean truly well? He has been through so much, and I cannot bear to imagine him suffering even more. Even at this moment, I worry for him, that he has yet again got himself caught in some scheme in search of a way out which will only bury us all the more. Or worse, bury himself and leave me to watch.'

'Virginia, to speak with full truth, I am not sure that one can ever fully recover from the things your love has seen. But I can tell you, there are worse things in the world. The bitch he speaks of so distastefully can beat him, drain him of blood, any of those horrific things... but when the sun sets, the body begins to heal. So far in my life, I am not convinced the soul, though, can heal. And whether or not Martin has incurred experience which has stepped on his soul—I do not know. That is something only the man himself can speak of.'

'You talk as you too have been hurt in the soul.' I found this comment to be practically laughable. What lies in plain sight may seem normal, but what is normal is often that which is best hidden.

'Virginia, look at me. Look at me clearly. Take a step back and look at me if you must. For you to think that I have not had my soul torn at is practically an insult—how ignorant to reality you would need to be!'

'Hannah... I'm sorry. I surely did not mean to...'

I made a conscious choice to continue talking over her.

'But I think there remains another essential distinction to be drawn, and that is that; while I am yet to have seen the soul heal, that does not mean that my mind is closed off to the idea. In fact, nothing would make me happier than to watch souls heal. Souls are the fabric of existence, if you will. To heal a soul is to mend a life. And to mend a life... what more can be asked for? Every day, I pray that souls might be mended, and that some little thread, regardless of its size, finds its way back together. Maybe that is why I do what I do, now that I think about it. Maybe it is the truth which mends the soul, and, conversely, lies which tear it apart... If I seek the truth, then am I a mender of souls? Wouldn't that be fantastic responsibility? To help the hurt back to wholeness would be the most selfless and rewarding task one could ask for... but I digress into the abstract. You husband is hurt—very much physically, but also, there is a real possibility that his injuries conceal themselves in plain sight. I have not seen the man act too disfigured or hurt recently, but that is not to say that an... internal injury is out of the question. In fact, an internal injury is quite in the question. I do not believe that one goes through what that man has and comes out unscathed. He shows no pain outwardly. But I bet you my life's savings that he is crippled on the inside.'

'Oh! What will I do?' The tears which had been welling in her eyes while I spoke finally burst and streamed down her face. They were silent tears, but very real, and full of sorrow and pity and... angst? My response to her question was not verbal, but physical. In that moment, nothing could bring the poor soul more comfort than the love of another.

I still recall reasons that her concerns were justified, and that Virginia did indeed have very good reason to doubt the man. But she was never made aware of these reasons—at least not under my supervision for the remainder of the day. I suspect that she never will be made aware either. Her naiveté serves her well.

*Evening in Paradiso*—We arrived in Paradiso at 5:00. The sun was beginning to approach the end of its cycle that day, and its horizontal rays penetrated the city in the west, flew through, and burst out the east. The whole town was erected around one fountain in the shape of a compass rose, with four streets: Norori Rd, Austri Ave, Suori Ln, and Vestri Blvd all intersected at the fountain. If one was unaware of the fountain's particularly violent nature, they could enjoy their time in Paradiso. Locals informed me, quite kindly, that in the winter, snow would fall, but never too much. It would come in the perfect quantity so that the children could build their snow forts, but the adults would not need to scrape roads. In the fall, unlike the rest of the mountains, the trees in Paradiso would turn red—and orange and yellow, like the rolling hills of the eastern seaboard. Children would form large piles of leaves and jump in and out of them with great enthusiasm. When the summer came, the mountain snow would melt, and small streams flowed on the outskirts of the town, where families would frolic together, throwing their children into their air with smiles mounted on their faces. The cool mountain water would settle the dust down. And when it rained, the earth drank in all the water which fell onto its face, so there were no floods.

But this was by day.

At night, the town became a different place. The

restaurants which so happily hosted families and relatives donned to their evening clothing. The waitresses left their posts so that the prostitutes and bartenders could take them. The husbands and fathers, who by day labored intensely for the affection of their wives and children, descended in swarms. The smell of the town changed, regardless of whether it was the smell of snow, flowers in bloom, pine trees, or rotting leaves by day, to a smell which stung the nose and reeked of the devil, in the night. The woman clung to their children, burying their faces in the women's breast so that the seductive scent of the devil would overlook them.

But again, it is only the collective word of a hodgepodge of locals—a smattering of stories from a peculiar series of interactions at a saloon; I believe that is what they are called here. But this particular series of interactions began in a curious way, because when we arrived in town, without Martin, we quickly found Martin—in the saloon. All of a sudden, Ms. Kelly's temperate love resembled a drunkard at a fair. It was the evening; Art, Virginia, and I set out to familiarize ourselves with our surroundings. Needless to say we were well aware of the illicit nature of the indulgences around us. Speakeasies littered the streets, and sober men entering them refused to pick up the rubbish.

One raucous scene inside of the saloon in question caught our attention from the streets when inebriated fanatics began hurling insults at one another:

'Goddamned Bible bumper! Get your nose out of here!'

'Get your head out of the clouds, you bimbo! You will not find the Lord there! Only through prayer!'

Another voice spoke: 'Maybe he's one of 'em Holy Rollers. They've been comin' 'round a lot more as of recent.'

This religious altercation piqued the interest of Art, who was a self-proclaimed theologian. Dragging our attention by the collar, he took us into the bar, and much to our surprise, to our left were the fanatics, to our right were the missionaries, but smack-dab in the middle of it all was Martin. Although his back was turned to us, he wore the same green overcoat from the train. It was, however, matted with a noticeable amount of dust, as if the man himself had gotten into an altercation. Unfortunately for Virginia, his presence was her first observation. And when she called his name, if Martin had spun around with a slightly lessened radius, he may not have revealed the amber beverage on the counter.

'What... what... what is that?' Her lips quivered and her pointer finger shivered as she raised it towards the glass. I turned my face to her ear and whispered quietly.

'I think that we should make our exit, now.'

Virginia, however, could not contain herself, and shouted: 'No! No!'

She succeeded in drawing everyone's attention to herself. The fanatics and missionaries stopped bickering and Martin sat on the stool, wide-eyed and wordless. He moved his lips as if to speak but nothing came out.

Yet again, tears came to the poor woman's eyes. How volatile her emotional state had been in the last few days...

'What is that?' No response. 'I demand an explanation. I have done nothing but care for you Martin, and you turn around, behind my back and violate our—no, I suppose only my—principles. I uprooted my life for you and traveled across the country for heaven's sake... and this is what I get in return? A drunken partner who I cannot even trust to uphold basic principles of decency. It is truly abominable. Explain yourself. I demand to know... why, you detestable fools!'

'Dear, you don't know the troubles I've seen.' This, he whispered to the ground. Then he erupted into yell, clearly impaired in his judgement: 'You don't know the troubles I've seen. And you never will.' His anger gave way to a quivering lip and tearing eyes. 'I have done everything for... for you! And this is what I get? How dare you try to impose your own principles upon me. I have labored for you, relentlessly. I think I deserve leniency in these matters.' He stood up from the stool and made his way towards where the three of us stood. For every step he took towards Virginia, she shrunk into her shell, until Martin stood an arm's length away and her hands were pressed tight against her breast. He again spoke softly, though now with force—a voluminous whisper. 'I hope that you'll consider my sovereignty in this matter. It is unfortunate that you think that we, as lovers, need to share our experience uniformly, and that neither of us can have autonomy in the matter.' Art shuffled closer to the void between them, to stop any inter-relationship altercation which might erupt at a moment's notice.

Virginia's voice rose an octave and her eyes were red with tears: 'I don't want uniformity, just transparency in the matter. I want an honest husband, who respects the rule of law and... me! Is that too much? Is it?'

Martin stared at her for a minute, before releasing the grasp imposed by his glare. He then spoke to Art and me: 'I hope the two of you will have the decency to show Ms. Kelly to a room at some local... brothel. As for us, we'd better meet in two hours at the fountain... The plane landed this morning... earlier than we expected.'

I had somehow earned myself a spot among the group of individuals going to capture the Aesternas, on the grounds of my being a journalist. I did, however, concede that I would under no circumstance put myself in harm's way. Virginia, quite apparently, was not invited, which made the short walk back to the hotel quite awkward. This was compounded only by the fact that the man whom she had practically devoted her life had accosted her in the worst way.

The Valhalla Inn was quaint. There were ample bedrooms, all located on the ground floor. Virginia had served her time. It is only my hope that her ardent values might have had some meaningful impact on Martin; though, in his drunken state, I am afraid that her principles might not resonate as much as any of us would have liked. The energy had been taken from her by the conquest of her values—and her righteous desire to spread them.

Inside the room was a single bed, very well-made. The whole room was sterile. The ceilings were high, and a single yellow bulb fell from the apex. The only hint of decoration was a small painting opposite the bed of a castle. The fortress stood on a bluff, and a grand waterfall shot outward from under it. Above, the clouds parted and made way for the sun's rays, which cast a shadow onto the water below.

Once Virginia was settled, Art and I set off for the fountain. We walked down Austri Ave towards the fountain, and into the setting sun. But large, voluminous clouds eclipsed the sun. The clouds stood like a fortress. But whether we were in the fortress protected from the setting sun, or the sun was in the fortress protected from us, I could not discern. That is often the problem, I have found, with fortresses of such immense size. It is often difficult to tell who is on the right side of things, and if there is even a right side of things. In theory, everyone believes they are on the right side of the walls: either attacking that which is wrong, or defending that which is right. The objectively correct choice is almost always subjective in nature.

Unlike the many awkward meals we had eaten recently as a group of three and four, the conversation between us was quite natural, and we spoke with confidence. But as Art spoke, there was a hint of utter defeat, or anticipation of defeat in his voice.'

'Hannah, do you remember when we were young and you would come to my house?'

'Yes, I suppose I do. What of it?'

'I was ready to die, and I think you saved me.'

'I'm much flattered, but I don't see how I did anything of the sort.'

'Hannah, perhaps you haven't realized, but you entered my life and filled a void. Only days before I met you, I killed my parents. Think about that for a moment. It was not even a novel murder of a stranger. I ended the life which bore me. Think about how miserable and hurt one needs to be to slay their creator and guardian.'

There was silence as I pondered the magnitude of what he suggested. He spoke again.

'Do you recall how after the Father was moved, I disappeared shortly after? Did you ever wonder what happened to me?'

'I suppose I've had the thought, but what does it matter now that you are beside me and I am here?'

'Hannah, I was just a boy thrust into the jaws of life, even before you entered it. But the impact you had on me was immeasurable. I was... broken within, and you healed me, perhaps without even noticing it. That is the nature of good, I have found. The most good is done when do-gooders don't even realize they are doing good—when it is so perfunctory that it's natural. When I left Baltimore, I wandered around the country. I wandered west and north and south. I found a wealthy farmer in Illinois who took me in. They cared for me well and saw that I was healthy. There was no emphasis on education, and I existed with them more as an employee than a child. But they did good, even when they did not realize they were doing it. They saw to my well-being, even when, at times, they became quite flustered by the attention I occasionally required. And I returned the favor. The man died when he was twenty-four, and left the old woman, Mrs. Jeffjen. I became the soul plower of land for her, doing one day's work for four men in the matter of a morning. When her time came to climb to the spirit in the sky, I sat beside her and held her hand. and she said to me: "Never wrangle with your words, my boy. Let them be free like the stallions in the pasture. I reckon I know the fate of the world as clearly as any of us. You have done a great deal of good in your life, and I thank you for it... Ah, here comes that hand; it is my time." Only when I had done my share of good in the world did I return to the East and begin my current profession.'

'Art, I'm humbled and moved, by what you have to say, but I don't see how this pertains to the situation at hand.'

'I say this only to point out the overt good you're doing—quite willfully I might add. Hannah, perhaps you have not thought of it yet, but we may very well pass on to the next life tonight. There is no doubt in my mind that blood will be shed. Aren't we all just dust? Tonight, I am persuaded that to the dust someone shall return.'

'Art, that is a grim thought! You would do well not to put such eschatological imagery in my head prior to such an operation.'

'I mean no harm—none at all. But I think we must arm ourselves—in the moral sense, of course. Fate is like an invisible rope; it bends to our will—to some degree. But it cannot be pulled apart. And even if we pull it apart, strand by strand, it will always find its way back together; some ethereal being will make sure of that.'

As he finished the sentence, the fountain came into view. Martin stood, having clearly vomited on himself several times, against the fountain. There was a small band of mercenaries with him, largely, it would appear, the forest people sent by Mam. Each of them held a sizable firearm, and looked at me with more than a pinch of contempt. Their faces were ovular, but not in the direction one would expect, with fat lips and plumb-like noses. There were wagons Martin had arranged for to carry us most of the way before he became the drunken man we witnessed only hours before, I assume.

We loaded into the wagons. As we set off up Norori Rd, I looked, for the last time that night, at the sun down Vestri Blvd. The clouds had parted ever so slightly, to give me one last glimpse of the sun as it kissed and sunk into the horizon.

# XXIII

DIARY OF HANNAH HERRMAN

*June 26th (on the events of the evening of June 25th)*—Below is a story of fate, not told lightly. There is death and sadness and mourning and victory. It is shrouded in mystery and largely will remain as such until the end of time.

Once the sun had set and the wagons had taken us as far as had been previously, we dismounted and moved forward into the murky woods on foot. We had travelled for many hours north, and the time, while not clear, was late. We came to a small clearing, and gesturing for silence, a still drunk Martin belligerently told us all to crouch to the ground. Shimmying forward, we realized that we laid on the top of a ridge, overlooking a lengthy valley. The forest below looked equally murky, and even the pointy tops of the trees struggled to pierce the damp quilt which hung above them. The air was wet like we were submerged in a lake, and the ripples of our breath could almost be made out. The whole scene was quite mysterious.

But perched on a bluff in the distance, overlooking the misty and drenched forest, was a large house—the House of Aesterna. After focusing on it for a moment, the facade became quite clear. Facing us were several large windows, meant to provide a panoramic view of the valley. But, like I have written before, only when we are hidden do the most poignant of secrets often reveal themselves. I removed a miniature spyglass from my satchel and telescoped it outward. No one else, of the twenty or so bearded, woodland men lying flat on the ferns and being shat on by the tree squirrels and birds had a luxury of similar comparison.

But what I spied through my telescoping glass is a story I still have not told to the others—for I am not sure what reaction it could possibly incite. We laid there, flush with the ground for several hours before this particular... performance occurred. At this time, Martin spoke, more gregarious than ever due to his goosed nature.

'In the coming hours,' he softly proclaimed, 'brothers will struggle and slaughter each other, and sisters' sons spoil kinship's bonds. It's hard on earth: great whoredom; axe-age, blade-age, shields are split; wind-age, wolf-age, before the world crumbles: No one shall spare another!' It became quite clear that Martin had never intended, even in part, to honor his promise to Virginia. The bastard knew he was already bound to the lowest level in hell from the outset, so why not deceive a skosh more; he had already committed treachery. He continued: 'The wood of destiny is kindled, my friends, and we shall advance close, though hidden, and when the ancient horn casts its call throughout the valley, we shall lay siege to everything they have.'

Martin's speech was alluring to the brutes in the group, successfully rallying courage, though I paid it little interest. They beat their calloused hands on the ground in support of the demagogue, but I remained in my position, largely out of sight and out of mind of the men. They were angry, and their anger distracted them from Martin's inner rage.

When his battle cry continued, Art came and laid beside me, his torso propped up by his elbows, which pressed into the dirt.

'Anything of interest that you've seen?'

'Not too much, I think—' But as I spoke, that changed quickly. Peering through the spyglass, I witnessed an execution of the most brutal nature. 'Give me one moment, Art.' I spoke calmly as to not alert him to the throbbing nature of my heart or the clammy moisture of my palms. This is as best as I can describe the ritual:

Two tall and burly individuals dragged a man out from house left. The men in their late twenties dressed in fine apparel—bow ties, jackets, gloves, and such. Each had a hand on the collar of the human form being dragged between them, with a canvas bag over their face, tightly cinched by twine at the throat. He wore a blue jacket and was thrust to his knees by the large men on either side of him in the center of the panoramic windows. One of the men, with no lack of boiling vehemence, severed the twine and pulled out the canvas bag from his head.

It was none other than Ozirus Aesterna. Though I had never seen the man in the flesh prior to this moment, he had the horizontal scar on his cheek and a cock-eyed nose like Martin had described when I spoke with him in the hospital. The man who I had written about and followed, if only indirectly, for months, was on his knees, bleeding from below the left eye. And I was the only sane person who knew anything of it. Eventually he looked up at another figure who was entering from house right. But this was a woman—none other than Ekaterina. I could hardly believe my eyes. I pulled back from the eyeglass for a moment, to extract myself from the grotesque performance.

Because of the darkness, we failed to observe the entrance of clouds into the scene above us. The rain came with the clouds—first a light haze, then drops. The boom of thunder in the distance resonated throughout the valley.

More than ever, little bouts of life became prominent. Though it was dark, the grass looked lush and the pine needles smelled more vibrant than ever. A small centipede flowed across my field of vision. Whereas if I had seen the creature only moments before, I may have practically had a severe chill and shrieked; I now stared at it with pity. Knowledgeable of my fear of the critters, Art reached over and squashed with his large thumb—he even smiled… the bastard. Water accumulated on the tips of pine needles and fell with great velocity towards the earth. These sights reeled my attention back towards the center stage of the household in the distance.

I returned my gaze to the performance before me.

Ekaterina approached the sorry man in her dark dress. She tried to bend down, but was prevented from doing so by her apparel. This made her reasonably embarrassed. No difference to her—the dress may have been able to restrict her movement, but not her malevolence. She slapped the poor man across the face, causing him to spit blood onto the floor, an act which she proceeded to patronize him for, pointing at the blood with cynical vigor. She exited the stage momentarily and returned with a long black hand-gun. She walked up to him and mercilessly struck him across the face with the gun. The poor soul keeled over, continuing to bleed out on his own floor.

The climax came quite nonchalantly when Ekaterina began to walk away from him. But at the last moment, she turned around, as if she had a sudden change of thought, and shot him—first in the chest, then forehead. The image became blurry as my hands shook spyglass. My breathing slowed. Despite the man's diabolic affiliation, I could not stand to see him die. In that moment, they were not bootlegger and wife, but victim and murderer—and for all they had done to harm others, I pitied the man.

I continued to watch the silent film through the spyglass. He continued to bleed onto the floor. In a short while, he laid in a pool of blood. His clothes and skin were stained red for eternity—for that is always how I will remember him; it is simply how I saw him the most.

What makes it all the worse is that the horror of the evening did not end there.

Shortly after waving Art away, so that I could think

to myself, Martin rallied the men. Refusing to be left behind, I walked through the forest below with the greatest respect for all the life around me, regardless of how misty or murky or diabolic it was. Large spiders danced across our path, but I simply watched them in amazement. How fragile it all was, and how quickly it could all be revoked. For two hours, we traversed the valley floor. The rain began to pour, but nothing could dissuade Martin, the fearless leader, so nothing would dissuade those who followed him. My thin shoes were soaked through and submerged in mud. Still in shock, I nearly tripped over branches and slipped in the mud, saved only by Art's careful watch. I avoided stepping on the shrubbery at all costs, and twisted my foot slightly after every step, in an attempt to not leave a footprint. Art's words rang true in my mind: we were dust, and to dust someone had returned—the first of three significant players, to my knowledge, that evening.

Now bound to complete silence, the party held up at the bottom of the bluff and dispersed. I remained with Marty, Art, and several others directly below the windows, which were several stories up from where we stood. The thunder boomed again; this time, much closer.

The silence was ominous, following the boom, and I was not sure what signal we were waiting for, since one had not been expressly communicated. But seconds after the silence set in, a signal came. When the sound of gunfire was peppered upon us, I was the last to react, and only did so when Art tugged me passionately behind a large tree. Though the gunfire was not in our direction, it was common knowledge that all flesh was now fair game—and that there would be no mercy.

The greatest bout of thunder I had ever heard momentarily stopped the peppering, as everyone in the valley looked up into the eyes of an angry god. A great bolt of lightning descended in slow motion from the clouds, slithering its way to earth. It ignited the air around it with white light, and the heat... so much heat. It finally found a tree and wrapped itself around like a serpent. It squeezed the tree tightly, until at last, the tree exploded in flames. The serpent had squeezed the life out of it. From my limited vantage point, I could see the fire begin to spread. It did so with great haste, mercilessly slithering from one tree to the next. The scene began to defy reality. The fire continued to spread, and the rain continued to pour. The thunder boomed, and the lightning continued to slither down tree after tree.

We continued to run up the hill towards the house. The gunfire drew closer to us; though, without a light, we remained largely out of view. The dense and smoky forest eventually gave way to a clearing. And opposite us was the door to the house. It was a large door, made all the more dramatic by the hellish light projected onto it by the flames which descended towards the house from behind. The wind had picked up amid the rainstorm. Seeing clearly that there were no armed individuals around us, I broke the silence, yelling at the top of lungs.

'We need to leave. The cars are down the hill. If we don't, the fire will consume us; we'll be piles of ashes mixed with the ash of trees if we don't get out now.' Martin turned around with a monstrous expression. His eyes were open wider than I'd seen them before. The light from the fire around us constricted his pupils to specks in his eyes, and the dust in the air made his eyes red, while the ash found its way to creases in his face. His greasy stubble was accented likewise, as it reflected the fiery light. After a moment, he growled, revealing his teeth, armed like a wolf's fangs, preparing to down its prey. He spoke with a cynical rasp.

'How dare you try to stop us now. We have come this far, and walked for a whole night through a forest, and now you want to leave? Unfathomable! No—we will fight if it means we die in the flames.'

Art attempted to reason with the beast: 'Marty,' he said pitifully, 'look at yourself, man! We are here to kill a criminal—there will be more chances; I guarantee you that. It may take time, but I promise you will have your moment.'

'No! No! This isn't about alcohol or liquor or other people. It's about me! And that bitch's vile actions towards me!' He broke into tears, the sad being. The wind whipped around his head and blew his hair over his eyes. His jaw hung, jutted forward towards Art and me. He stood slightly, panting, crying, and thinking. 'You all are welcome to leave, but for all I care you can die in flames.' With that, he turned around and marched towards the doors.

Despite the rain, the smoke became heavy. It was blown into our faces by the violent wind, shoved down our throats. The flames could now be seen approaching the house through the trees. Art and I scrambled down the path and located a suitable getaway vehicle. As he began to jerry-rig the automobile, I glanced back towards the clearing from which we had descended. The flames burst through the trees and onto the ground. They jumped across the clearing and ignited the roof of the port cochere; one of the primary faults of the entirely wooden structure was its high degree of flammability.

From where I sat in the car, I had a complete view of the length of the house, on the left, the clearing and entrance, and on the far right, the panoramic windows which opened to a large porch, also made of wood. We began to drive down the hill away from the flames, but as we did so, though we were slightly lower than the deck, it came fully into view. Closer to us, with his back turned, was Martin; he was hunched over in a bestial manner as we drove past. Across from him was Ekaterina—the same woman whom I had watched shoot her husband only hours before. But instantly they were out of sight, as the car passed to the protection of the forest.

Many times, since I caught a glimpse of the confrontation, I have imagined what they said to one another, and why Ekaterina had not simply shot the creature before her. It must have gone, I think, something like this:

'Rise again, yes, rise again, will you, my dust, after a brief rest? Immortal life, immortal life—will he who called you, give you?' Ekaterina spoke with vain excitement, drawing on the previous interaction between the two. 'To bloom again, you were sown! The Lord of the harvest goes and gathers in like sheaves us together, who will die.' She cast an awful smile towards him, fully aware of their fates.

Martin wildly retorted: 'Oh believe, nothing to you is

lost! Your own fate, yes your own, is what you deserve. Your own, what you have loved, what you have fought for!' To himself, Martin then thought: Oh believe you were not born for nothing! Have not for nothing, lived and suffered.

Ekaterina: 'What was created must perish, what perished, rise again! Cease trembling, Martin. Prepare yourself to live! Oh pain, you piercer of all things, from you, I have been wrested. Oh death, you conqueror of all things, now, you are conquered.'

'With wings which I have won for myself, in love's fierce striving, I shall soar upwards, to the light which no eye has pierced.'

'Then die shall I in order to live—rise again, yes, rise again. Will you strike me down in an instant? That for which you suffered? To God shall it carry us both!'

The fiery serpent burst through the doors of the house and opened its mouth. They turned to face the beast—one with an ambivalent glare, and the other with benevolent smile. The serpent consumed them both. As they moved through its body, their eyes and organs disintegrated. Their skin was scorched until it turned ash. And when the serpent passed, out of the dust they were taken, but to dust they did return.

# XXIV

## DIARY OF HANNAH HERRMAN

*July 5th*—The events at the end of the previous month called for a great deal of introspection. I will need someone or something to heal my soul, but I have not found it yet.

Similarly, by the events of June I was somehow bound to the West, and today marks my first day as a resident in the city of San Francisco. It is a pleasant place, with lots of rolling hills. The coastal water is much more cold than in Philadelphia, but the warmth from the Pacific Ocean must have infused the local air. Every morning, dense clouds give way to a placid scene of the sun and the ocean.

I also have an interview with The Chronicle today. The walk is quite convenient, only a few blocks from my Union Square flat. I hope sincerely that my pursuit for the truth can continue. It is a most curious quest, which, evidently, has brought me many troubles and lost me many friends.

Speaking of which, I am yet to have seen Virginia.

Shortly after we escaped the grasp of death, Art was reunited with his vagabond nature, roaming the west, but this time, with my location committed to memory. I have not seen Virginia since that evening. When Art and I returned to the hotel—soaked and burned and sad as we were—she nor her belongings were anywhere to be found. That is the peculiar nature of people: they are never where they want to be and are always where they loathe.

I have also procured an interesting painting by chance, conferred on me by a resident of Paradiso as we left. It was of a man clothed with a garment down to the foot and dressed about his chest with a golden girdle. His head and his hairs were white like wool, as white as snow; and his eyes were as a flame. It hung opposite by the bed in my new flat, and I have pondered it periodically since then.

SOUTH LAKE TAHOE TRIBUNE: 'BODY FOUND
WASHED UP ON SHORE'
Published June 30th, 1927

The body of a woman was discovered on the evening of Wednesday, June 29th. The women is currently unidentified due to the effects of water on the body's decomposition. She had jet-black hair, and she wore a white coat.

The cause of death has been determined to be drowning, and there are no indications of a struggle. This fact, combined with a lack of wounds, has led authorities to conclude this was a suicide. Another peculiar finding in the autopsy was the presence of ash in the victim's lungs, leading authorities to believe that the death may be linked to the forest fire which consumed all the land within 10.0 leagues from the bolt of lightning which initiated the fire in the east of Plumas National Forest.

Police speculate that the loss of a home, personal property, or a loved one may have served as motivation for the woman's death.

If you, or anyone you know, has any information connected to the death, please contact your local authorities as soon as possible.

## A NOTE FOUND BY WILDFIRE INVESTIGATORS IN A BOTTLE, PRESERVED IN THE REMAINS OF A BURNT HOUSE
### Found July 10th

So this is how it ends? I hope that hell is not too hot—for all our sakes.